3rd and
LONG

www.
frosthollowpub.com

Text set in Palatino
Copyright 2006 by Robert Holland
Printed on acid-free paper in Canada
ISBN 0 - 9720922-8-5

Frost Hollow Publishers,LLC
411 Barlow Cemetery Road
Woodstock, CT 06281
phone: 860-974-2081
fax: 860-974-0813
email: frosthollow@mindspring.com

www.
frosthollowpub.com

3rd and
LONG

A Charles Oliver Jones
Martha's Vineyard Mystery

Robert Holland

Books for Boys

by

Robert Holland

The Voice of the Tree
The Purple Car
Summer on Kidd's Creek
Footballs Never Bounce True
Breakin' Stones
Eben Stroud
Harry the Hook
Mad Max Murphy
The One-Legged Man Who Came Out of a Well
The Last Champion
Charlie Dollarhide
The Black Queen
Crossing the River
Stealing
Spooks
Rumors
3rd and Long
Hobson's Choice

Check your local bookseller or order directly from Frost Hollow. Call toll free at 877-974-2081. All titles are $12 except for *Spooks* and *3rd and Long* which are $15. Shipping and handling and sales tax extra.

www. frosthollowpub.com

1

The Thing In The Fog

Two nights before school started, I staked out Mrs. Parks' house to find out whether anyone was casing the place. If I seem a little doubtful that's because there have always been strange stories about Mrs. Parks, stuff like her interest in Caribbean religions, and in particular, voodoo, which was something I knew nothing about.

But I also knew her from the library. I had been checking out some books and she started a conversation about the books and after that, when we met, she'd suggest some others that I should read.

Sometimes we talked about the books and from those discussions I learned a lot about anthropology.

But there was no getting around her reputation and I think that's why the police didn't take her complaints seriously. But me? Hey, I need convincing and I decided to look into things. After all, Mrs. Parks was not one of those women who goes all weird over snakes and spiders.

Pete was a little more skeptical, but then he's only been my partner for a few months and he hasn't got the hang of being a detective yet. You have to be suspicious about everyone and everything. Still, like all athletes, he's deeply superstitious and I was planning on using that to convince him to watch the house on alternate nights.

Still, I didn't hold out much hope. He was getting ready for football and Pete is dedicated. During the season he doesn't party and he never stays up late. So any chance I had of getting my partner engaged in this enterprise depended on my seeing something.

It was not a good way to start. Far too often, when you have the need to see something, you end up convincing yourself that you have, in fact, seen something. That is what some folks call a slippery slope.

So there I was, dressed in a gray ninja suit, including a hood, sitting in the dark of the woods in a Martha's Vineyard fog so thick that at times I couldn't see thirty feet.

The house sits on something over two hundred acres at the end of a long dirt road. Mrs. Parks' grandfather bought the land long before the real estate prices on Martha's Vineyard shot up into the millions.

What I'm getting at here is that I had begun to feel a little edgy about the isolation, despite having a cell phone and several throwing stars. I'm not exactly helpless. I've got a black belt in Karate and I've been boxing since I was twelve. I'm also six feet tall and I weigh two hundred pounds. But sometimes things creep in and they're hard to chase out.

The other thing is, I'm not used to the woods. Private investigators are mostly city guys. In the woods you are absolutely alone and it wasn't something I had thought about 'til then, and it was making me a little edgy.

If it had that effect on me it would be worse for Pete, who never spent any time in places like this, and I was pretty sure he'd be nervous as a cat in coyote country.

An hour went slowly by. Midnight. A chilly night, which explained the fog, and in the damp dark I took a long, deep breath, let it out slowly and settled in for another half-hour. If nothing happened by then, I'd check with Mrs. Parks in the morning.

After another fifteen minutes, I realized that I had been operating on the assumption that nobody would try breaking in at the front of the house because of the road. As assumptions go, it wasn't all that bad, but I'd failed to consider how the fog changed things and how few people ever used this road. Stupid.

I eased myself to a standing position and slipped back into the pines and began slowly, a step at a time, working my way toward the road. The trick is to move as little of your body as possible. Motion is what alerts a predator and humans are predators. I tried to pretend that my upper body was as stiff as a tree trunk.

I heard nothing. I saw nothing. Finally, I took up station in a thick part of the woods, where it came in close to the end of the house. But this time I didn't sit down because I wasn't planning on staying long.

The sound was absolutely identifiable: the sound an aluminum storm window makes in its track, and it was close.

I took a deep breath, not liking my situation. The fog had thickened and I couldn't see more than ten feet so I had no idea who or what had moved the storm window. Well, I was pretty sure it wasn't a what, because the one thing we don't have on the Vineyard is much in the way of "whats"; things like bears for example, or, in fact any animal large enough to cause a human any trouble, especially one my size.

On the other hand, even ruling out the "whats" did not exactly spread calm. The "whats" don't carry guns and humans do. Another deep breath and then, keeping close to the ground, I closed the distance to the house and flattened myself against the wall. I eased my head around the corner so I could see along the front wall as a soft breeze slipped down from the roof and for an instant the fog thinned and I could see an enormous, humanlike figure trying to jimmy open the inside lock on the window.

I was working out my choices when suddenly the lights

came on in the house and the ... whatever it was ... turned and ran right at me. In the light I got a good look and pulled my head back out of sight as the figure came rushing toward me along the front wall of the house, heading for the thick woods beyond.

I wanted nothing to do with it, but something inside me made me stick out my foot as it reached the corner of the building and it let out a loud sort of grunt and tumbled out onto the lawn and I went after it, leaping into the air and smashing my foot into its head as it began to get up. It grunted again but my kick didn't even slow it down and it got onto its feet and one long arm slashed out at me and I felt something tear through my shirt as I leaped away. Then it stood up to its full height and I leaped back.

There was nothing to measure against but it had to be eight feet tall and maybe a yard wide. I couldn't move. I felt as if my feet had been nailed to the ground. I dropped into a fighter's crouch and waited.

Slowly, it stepped backward away from me and then sideways into the shadow of the house as the fog closed in again and I blinked my eyes several times. It was gone.

I heard it reach the woods and for an instant I considered following, but an ambush was way too easy because I would be moving fast and making noise, while he needed only to wait. I took a deep breath, straightened, and then took another deep breath. This was a case worthy of Charles

5

Oliver Jones ... though I had to admit that just then, I felt maybe a little overmatched.

But never, not for a second, did I consider quitting. I walked back to the front of the house and rang the bell.

"Who's there?" Mrs. Parks shouted, her voice very high and excited.

"It's me, Mrs. Parks, Charlie Jones."

"Who?"

"Charlie Jones. You asked me to check things out for you."

"Who? Oh, Charlie. Well, why didn't you say so?" She opened the door and I stepped inside. Mrs. Parks is close to six feet tall and big. Her hair is almost white and she doesn't get around all that well, but then she is also in her eighties.

In the summer, the house crawls with children and grand-children and great grandchildren, but in the off-season she's pretty much alone except for a small group of friends who meet for lunch nearly every day and play bridge a couple of nights a week.

"Was that you I heard out there?"

I shook my head. "Someone else. He opened the storm window and he was trying to jimmy the window lock."

"Now there! I told those cops that somebody was trying to break in and they wouldn't listen! Just think I'm some silly old woman, living alone, scared of every sound."

"I'll talk with the chief in the morning."

"Did you run him off?"

"He ran when you turned on the light. I almost had him."
Okay, it was an exaggeration, but in this business the client
has to have confidence in the investigator.

She pulled her head back and looked up at me with that
calculating look adults use on you when they're pretty sure
you're making something up.

"I tripped him and I got in one good kick and then the
fog closed back in."

She shook her head. "I'm supposed to believe that?"

I shrugged. "I don't think he'll be back tonight. Just keep
a light on in every room."

"What's this man look like?"

"He's pretty tall and wide."

"How tall?"

I hesitated. Should I tell her? What was to be gained?

"What are we talking here, Charlie? Six-six, six-seven?"

"About eight feet, I think."

"Maybe he only looked that tall."

I knew what she was thinking. And why wouldn't she
doubt me? Everyone exaggerates. "No," I said. "Eight feet,
maybe a little more."

"Huh. He white or black?"

"Couldn't tell."

"You must not have got a very good look, then."

"I saw him."

"Well?"

"He had some kind of a disguise on, I think, you know, like a ski mask or something."

"I think you're not telling me everything you saw, are you, Charlie?"

"It looked like an enormous bear." Then I remembered the slash it had taken at me and I looked down and across the front of my shirt were four distinct tears. "If I hadn't had a kevlar vest under my shirt I'd have been ripped wide open."

"It did that?" she asked, her eyes wide with disbelief.

I nodded. "I jumped back just in time."

"You certainly did," she said. "And now I think maybe I'll call those cops this very minute. You just sit down over there and we'll see what they have to say about this! All but calling me a liar … huh!"

2

I'm Off The Case

We got lucky. The cop on patrol was Walt Fears. He knew Mrs. Parks and, in fact, probably knew every winter resident in Edgartown. He's a sergeant on the force now and usually he doesn't work nights, but with two guys out sick he'd had to fill in.

Walt Fears is a good guy. Make no mistake here. Even in desperate situations he's always calm and he gets things done right. And you can bet that if Walt arrests you, you're probably guilty.

I took him outside and showed him the storm window and the marks on the sash where the thing tried to open the window. With his light we looked at the tracks in the soft dirt by the house and I have to say I was a little disappointed when they turned out to be boot tracks. I was also a little relieved. Chasing people is one thing but the thought of pursuing some kind of supernatural creature ... well, the way I saw it I wouldn't be comfortable with some weird movie coming to life.

On the other hand, those boots must have been a size twenty-five and anyone who wears boots that big is either very large or very weirdly proportioned.

The slashes in my shirt could be explained easily enough, I mean, anyone could make up some kind of device shaped like a bear claw and equipped with razor blades.

We sat in the living room, drinking coffee (I had hot chocolate because Mrs. Parks said she wasn't about to be serving coffee to a young man my age in the middle of the night).

"Velda," Walt said, "I'm not sure what to make of this." He grinned at her. "You didn't put a spell on anyone did you?"

She laughed and shook her head. "Walter, don't be draggin' up a lot of old rumors." But there was something in her voice that made me wonder whether it was rumor or not.

He nodded. "Well, you got somebody angry at you."

"Or maybe it's just a prank, somebody trying to scare me because I live all alone."

Walt looked around at me. "You think he'll be back tonight?"

I shook my head. "Nope. I don't think he expected any trouble."

"Your kick slow him down much?"

"About like a flea bite."

"How'd you know to jump back?"

"I saw his head move and I knew what was coming." I grinned. "Well, I didn't expect the claw part."

Walt shifted in the chair, the leather in his pistol belt and holster creaking softly. "Charlie, here's the thing. I'll be talking to Bart in the morning and I know he's gonna talk to your dad and you know what they're gonna tell you."

I grinned. "Stay out of it."

"And that's right," Mrs. Parks said. "You stay right out of this, Charlie Jones. I was wrong to ask you to take such a risk. When I think of that claw and what it might've done to you, I just shudder all over." She looked around at Walt. "But now somebody's gonna have to keep a watch."

"I'll see what Bart says," Walt said, "but I'd guess we'll be doing something. Not likely we'd let one of our oldest and most famous citizens face something like that."

Famous? I had no idea Mrs. Parks was famous. I made a note to check with Dad. Nobody had information about Vineyarders like Dad did. And it was all in his head. No notes. No pieces of paper someone could steal. A careful man.

Officially, I was off the case. But the truth is, I was never truly on the case because I don't have a license to investigate anything. Besides, just maybe I was a little outgunned here. Okay. No more stakeouts. But I had other plans. For one thing I was pretty sure that a pair of boots that size would have to be ordered and it would be easy enough to check the stores that sold shoes. Nobody would be likely to forget that.

Nor was there anything to prevent me from keeping an eye out for a man that size. And because this is an island it's usually a good idea to keep a watch on ferry passengers, except that anyone could stay in their car and never be seen except driving on and off the boat. But even then, when he drove on at Woods Hole and handed over his ticket, anyone that size would have huge hands and that would be hard to miss ... unless he was a passenger.

At least I could mention it to Bart and he could talk to the guys who took tickets. My bet was that he'd already covered that. He's pretty sharp about things like that. But he does have one shortcoming. He tends not to believe something until he's got some hard evidence. In part that has to do with having to run his department on a tight budget and with not a whole lot of people.

What I hoped was that Walt would be able to convince him. He listened to Walt. I knew that because Dad had told me. Bart and Walt relied on each other. It was a good place to start.

3

Football Begins

The next morning football practice started and there I was dressed in shorts, a t-shirt, and cleats, which meant no contact. Coach Walton separated us into two groups: those who had played the year before and the new guys.

Pete had told me what to expect, and from the way the other guys behaved, I guessed they had informers as well. Most of them were sophomores and I was the only new guy who was a senior.

It started with calisthenics. No problem. I worked out all the time and I ran and I was in good shape. It even felt good to be out there in the bright late August sunshine with a bunch of guys, sweating, and for the first time in my life being part of something.

Pete might think I could make the team, but I wasn't so

sure. I'd never played football or any other team sport and I had no idea how to react to the coach and his assistant. They sounded tough and unforgiving, which made sense, seeing as the game was football and anybody who wasn't willing to hurl himself into another player with no regard for his body parts wasn't gonna make the team.

Body parts don't matter in football. You expect to get hurt. You expect to get shouted at and called names. And then you shower up, go home and can't wait for the next practice. I'd read that somewhere, or maybe I'd heard it in an interview and I had never doubted it was true.

The last item on the calisthenic list was push-ups. You had to do twenty. Again. No problem. I could do a hundred. The way it worked, you did twenty and if you could do more, you kept going until only one guy was left.

At thirty-two I was still going and I was alone. So I quit at fifty and stood up, figuring it wasn't smart to make all those other guys look bad on the first day.

From the corner of my eye I could see Coach looking me over and then making a note on his clipboard, and I wondered if Pete had tipped him off. It seemed likely but he hadn't said anything, and in a way, I hoped he hadn't.

The last thing we did was run forty yards against the stopwatch and man, did that separate the sheep from the goats. You'd have thought that some of those guys had never run more than ten yards in their` whole lives.

They were panting and wheezing and a couple of guys even puked, which, I gotta say, was pretty ugly, though the coaches didn't seem to take any notice.

At the far end of the field I could see the rest of the team, going through various drills, running through rows of car tires laid flat, stop and go drills, and windsprints, and it seemed to me that they were working harder than we were.

But when it came to the forty-yard run everyone came together. The list was alphabetical and when the coach called for Dollarhide I watched carefully. Everyone in school knew about Charlie Dollarhide. As a freshman, he'd broken the state record in the hundred meter. And over the summer he'd done some growing. He was about five-nine now and he'd filled out quite a bit and I wondered if that would slow him down.

It didn't. It took him two steps to reach full speed and then he shot down the field as if he were rocket propelled. But then, some guys just know how to run and I guess maybe you have to be born to it. If it were any other way, then everyone could learn to run that fast and everybody knows that isn't true.

Five or six guys later my turn came and I stepped to the line and when the coach said GO! I shot away from the line and pumped as hard as I could.

Pete had said I was fast, but I figured that compared to Dollarhide I was a turtle. But to tell you the truth, I didn't feel even slightly turtelish. I was trying to cover the distance in under 5.0 and I came in at 4.7. Dollarhide did it in a flat 4.0. Three of us had made it in under five seconds and the other guy was Caleb Strong, who ran it in 4.9. He's our running back. Pete came in at 5.0 but then nobody expects a quarterback to run like a wide receiver. Still, I thought maybe I could jab him a couple of times about running like a snail.

By the time we finished the morning practice, I had begun to think I might have a shot. And then I began to think about getting hit and I wondered. You could be in great shape and run like the wind but that didn't mean you wouldn't cave when some guy came crashing into you.

I met Pete at the Microbus.

"Well?" he asked as I climbed in.

"Well what?" I said.

"I told you you were fast."

"Who knew?"

"Me! I knew."

"Dollarhide did it in four-0."

"Of course he did. He's the fastest kid in the whole state."

"And he can catch the ball?"

"I've been working with him over the summer."

"Well, at least it takes more than one wide receiver." I tried not to sound discouraged, but, in truth I was. After all there were still the guys from last year.

"We'll be running passing drills this afternoon."

"I know."

"You'll see. I didn't feed you a line of crap, Charlie. You're the tallest, toughest guy at the position. Just not the fastest, but not by a lot. What, seven tenths of a second?"

I smiled. "I still think it'll take a miracle."

"Isn't that what you do best?"

I laughed. "Keep the compliments coming."

"Tomorrow we put the pads on. Then it begins to feel like football."

We rode quietly for a short way and then hit the A&P traffic. You can wait a long time in that traffic, though in another week, once we got past Labor Day, it would ease off considerably as most of the summer people fled for home.

"I had an interesting night last night," I said.

"Oh?"

I told him what had happened at Mrs. Parks's house, staying with the facts and not making it anything more than it was. But in fact, a big — whatever it was — was roaming the Island and I couldn't get around that.

"You're kidding, right?"

I shook my head. "I saw him ... or it ... or whatever."

"That is so sick! You think we could catch him?"

"Do we want to catch him?"

"Don't we?"

"Maybe if we're carrying something in three-o-eight."

"What's that?"

"Rifle cartridge ... seven point six two NATO."

"Whoa ... you think he's that dangerous, huh?"

"I don't know. All I know is that something that wears a size twenty-five boot and stands about eight feet tall is not something you want to go after unless you're well prepared. And unless I've missed something, I don't think anyone will be real happy about us lugging rifles around."

Pete is a true football player. He figures he can take anybody. But he can't. No one can, even if it helps to believe that when you're on the field.

"Anyway, we're off the case, at least officially."

"But you're still gonna do some poking around?"

"Safe stuff. See if anybody sold a pair of boots that big."

"What else?"

"I'm gonna ask Bart if I can go through all the complaints they've had for six months or so."

"He'll let you do that?"

"My guess is he's already doing it."

"Isn't Mrs. Parks some kind of religious weirdo?"

"Naw. That's just gossip. She has a degree in anthropology and her specialty is Caribbean religions. But she goes to church every Sunday in a regular church." And then I remembered what Walt Fears had said about her casting spells and the strange artwork on the walls of her house. It hadn't connected before, but now ... well you could never afford to overlook anything and I decided it might be a good idea to ask her, once I figured out how to do that without sounding like a complete idiot.

"Voodoo," Pete said. "They practice Voodoo in Haiti."

"Do you know anything about Voodoo?"

"Isn't there something about the living dead?"

"I don't know. I never read anything about it," I said.

"Well, maybe we oughta hit the library on the way back to practice and see what we can find."

"Sure."

"Yeah. This is gonna be fun. I love mysterious stuff like this."

What a private eye does is gather information. The more the better. But the great trick is not to convince yourself that it means anything until it all points in one direction. Easier said than done. Just like football. Well ... just like anything, I guess.

4

Back To Practice

Pete's got a tremendous arm and his throws are accurate. He's also got Division One size at six-four and two-twenty-five. And he's got quick feet that allow him to take a five or seven step drop into the pocket, or avoid the defense by slipping to the side. The other thing about Pete is that he never seems to rattle no matter how heavy the pressure.

Syracuse, Boston College, and UConn were already talking to him and there would be others, but that was pretty good for a start.

The thing is, a guy with ability like Pete's is about as rare as hen's teeth. Maybe once in a hundred years a high school gets a player like that.

What was really strange is that the spring before we'd had another one, a pitcher named Rob English. He went right into the minors after he graduated and he'd had a spectacular summer. He never lost a game, he threw four no-hitters and he was moving up to Triple-A, which is one step below the majors. And get this, he wouldn't be nineteen until the next spring.

The effect on me isn't hard to figure out. It was way, way beyond the law of averages that another great player would turn up, though I had a lot of hope for Charlie Dollarhide.

The bottom line is that at best I would just be an average player. It was not an idea I liked. I didn't like being average at anything, but you probably know that by now.

We stopped at the library and took out five books on Voodoo and then headed for practice.

"You think this thing really exists?" Pete asked.

"I saw it."

"But are you sure about what you saw? You said it was foggy and dark."

"I got one good look. Remind me when we get home and I'll show you my shirt with the slashes in it."

"Are the cops gonna put out a warning?"

"Not a chance, man."

"But why not? Doesn't it make sense?"

"They're afraid everybody would get way overheated and some perfectly innocent person would get shot."

"I can see that," Pete said. "I mean, who wouldn't wanna

be the guy who shot it?"

"We just have to see what happens."

"Are you gonna stake out Mrs. Parks' house again?"

"I'm thinking about it."

He laughed and banged the steering wheel. "I knew it! I knew you weren't gonna let them chase you off."

"I'm only thinking about it," I said.

"Okay, but I want to be there too. I mean, we put a pretty good hurt on those hoods out at Menensha, right?"

I grinned. "Yeah, we did." And indeed, we had, but that was no reason to let ourselves start thinking we were in the least way invincible.

After all, part of the reason we'd taken those guys down was that we'd used the element of surprise. Here's the thing. I'd taken the Thing in the Fog (which is what I was calling it, for lack of something better) by surprise and it had made absolutely no difference.

With any ordinary human being that kick would have just about taken his head off.

Afternoon practice did a lot to convince me that my chances of making the team were pretty good, or at least better than I had thought.

The quarterbacks and receivers, which included the running backs, worked at one end of the field while the meat worked at the other end. And they had another assistant now,

Mr. Klotts. You may have heard of him. Ormand Klotts, one of the best defensive secondary men the NFL ever saw. He was retired now and living here on the Island and he'd volunteered to coach our defensive secondary.

Football, if I haven't mentioned it before, is a big deal on the Vineyard. We get huge crowds and lots of people travel to our away games, all of which start with a ferry ride to get to the mainland. It means you gotta be dedicated, because even with the special islander rate, the ferry is expensive.

Maybe, to understand how it works, you have to live here year 'round. When the summer people leave, business slacks off considerably. Most of the summer stores close after Labor Day. We get our island back and it becomes a small town once again because the population density drops. There are about fifteen thousand people spread over 128 square miles. Everyone either knows everyone else or they know of them ... except for the new people who retire here. Mostly they seem to know each other and sometimes you feel like they would rather not associate with the natives. Fine with us. Just spend your money and keep quiet.

At first we ran simple slants, the receiver running up the field about ten yards and then cutting to the middle to catch the pass.

Pete had one group and the second group had the two sophomore quarterbacks, Ward Brooklyn and Twig Kellums.

And I guess because I was new, I started off with the second group, as did Charlie Dollarhide.

The two quarterbacks were in trouble with either one of us. We were both too fast and they couldn't get the timing down so their throws were considerably behind us. I managed to reach back and snag a few but only because I've got really long arms.

Three times we ran the drill and then Coach moved Charlie and me up to Pete's group.

Man did we have fun. Charlie has great hands and Pete had no trouble judging his speed.

We flew through the afternoon, neither of us dropping a pass and it didn't matter whether we were diving to the ground to catch a short pass or running a fly, either down the sideline or a post pattern down the middle.

Charlie had been well coached and so had I and we always worked as if we had a defenseman right on us, faking and spinning to make sure we could get a step on our imaginary defenders.

By the end of practice Charlie and I had become pretty good friends, but then he's an easy guy to like. He's got straight black hair and bright blue eyes and he's always smiling and laughing. He can even laugh at himself, which is not exactly a common trait in teenagers, present company included. I'm working on it.

The other thing about Charlie, who instantly became

known as C.D., is that he doesn't pretend he's something he isn't. He was there to play football. And so was I.

To do that I had to stay focused. Each time I lined up to run a pass pattern I made a picture of the ball dropping into my hands and then I focused on making that happen.

Each time it got easier. But of course I had Pete throwing the ball to me. Maybe you have to see that to understand just what an arm he has. It's a rifle ... an accurate rifle, and yet the ball doesn't feel heavy when it hits your hands.

I'd watched plenty of football on television and they talk a lot about quarterbacks throwing a light or a heavy ball. Until I caught Pete's passes, I didn't understand what that meant.

Here's what happens, a light ball is easier to catch, which means that if the ball comes in behind you, it's possible to reach back and snag it with one hand. A heavy ball is more likely to bounce off.

I think the explanation lies in the study of physics. Or maybe there is no answer. Maybe it's just one of those things you know to be true but can't explain.

In that way it was like whatever it was that had taken to roaming around in Mrs. Parks's woods.

5

A Visit With Mrs. Parks

After dinner I went to visit Mrs. Parks. I mean, nobody said I couldn't pay an ordinary social call, though I suspected Chief Espinoza would have frowned on it. And, of course, by then my folks knew what was up, which meant I told them I was going over to Pete's. They probably wondered why I drove but I figured I'd cross that particular river of fire when someone lit it.

"Why, Charlie, what are you doing here?" Mrs. Parks stood in the open doorway, pretty much filling it. "I thought you weren't supposed to be doing this anymore."

"I'm not," I said, "but I had a couple of questions."

"Well, come on in and make yourself at home. You want a soda or something?"

"No thanks. I just finished dinner."

We sat in the living room in big, comfortable chairs and I looked around at the pictures of her family hung in groups on the walls. It was a big family and not just in numbers. Everyone was tall and I mean tall! But then both of her sons had played in the NBA where even the guards are six-six.

"Now, what was it you wanted to know?"

I turned away from the pictures. "The man I saw the other night ..."

"If it was a man ..."

"For now, let's just say it was, okay?" I smiled. "The other possibility is kind of scary."

"You got that right."

"Have you ever heard about anything like this before?"

She looked at me, her eyes narrowing as she considered my question. "How should I answer that? Hummm, well, maybe the honest way is the best way. I've got no proof, you understand, got nothing but an old legend from my grand-father, who was the one first bought this land.

"He was a lawyer up in Boston, one of the first success-ful black lawyers. Went to Harvard for all his education and he made a lot of money and not just defending black people in court, because he wouldn't have made any money doing that in those days. He specialized in setting up corporations and finding financing for them, and he was very good at it. He'd heard about the Vineyard and one day he caught the packet boat in Boston and landed at Edgartown.

27

"He liked what he saw and he found a man who sold real estate and they went out looking at land. When he saw this land he bought the whole thing. Nearly five hundred acres all along the shore of Edgartown Great Pond. Land wasn't worth a whole lot here then and nobody saw the value of land on a body of water that wasn't open to the sea.

"But Grandpa did. Not only was he a smart man but he could see the value in things. He built this house and came every summer after that for at least a month and he kept the family here the whole summer.

"He had the whole piece surveyed and marked off in five acre lots so he could sell them when the price got high enough. But nothing happened for a long, long time. Not till after the first war. Times were good then, after Harding cut taxes, and people were looking for summer homes. Most of them chose the Cape, but others settled here and Grandpa sold a number of lots and then he stopped, saying the rest could wait until he could get more for each lot. He still had well over half the land left.

"Now, this is the part that's hard to understand. What he said and why he did what he said, turned out to be two different things. My father told me this."

She shifted in the chair and leaned toward him. "My father never told anyone else, so far as I know, and to this day I don't know why he told me.

"Grandpa used to love to walk. He walked the beaches

and he walked all through the woods. He hunted those woods every fall for deer and he was always successful. And then suddenly, one fall, in the middle of the season, he stopped. He just put his rifle into the closet and that was that. We asked, but we got no answer.

"What my father said is that he had been out hunting in the western section when he saw what he thought was a very large man drifting quietly through the woods. For awhile he followed, wanting to identify who it was that thought he could hunt this land without permission.

"He was an excellent hunter and despite his size, he was six-nine, he could move very quietly and he stayed behind the man for a long ways. For awhile, after the man went over a rise, he lost sight of him and then when Grandpa came up onto the rise, he moved very slowly, knowing that he would be easily seen at the crest of the hill, despite the trees.

"But the man had stopped just over the hill, waiting for him, and he took Grandpa completely by surprise, and suddenly he was standing not twenty feet away from something that was close to eight feet tall.

"They stood there, looking at each other for some time, neither one of them able to tell much because by then it was growing dark and there was a storm coming so the light was poor. What he saw, according to my father, was like nothing he had seen before. It looked like it was half man and half bear. It had a human face covered with dark hair as was the rest of it. The hands were just like ours, but they were enormous and covered with hair.

But the amazing thing was its eyes. They glowed with intelligence and Grandpa told my father he had the feeling that the creature could see right into his mind.

"They never took a step toward each other and Grandpa kept his rifle at his side. He was not a man to fear anything and his curiosity was powered by an enormous intellect. And when you're a human, you have to try speaking.

" 'Who are you?' he asked.

"That's when Grandpa began to understand. He was looking at a sasquatch, a legend, a myth that exists worldwide and is as old as time.

"Still, it didn't move. It made no sound, and what Grandpa said later was that it didn't have to. It meant him no harm and in fact, he remembered later, he felt safe.

"Grandpa smiled, took a step backward, and then another and that's when it moved away, going so fast it seemed to vanish into the air itself."

She sighed. "There were other sightings around that time and you can look them up in old copies of the newspaper. Grandpa was determined to find out whether he was right about what he had seen and he talked to everyone he could find and spent considerable time talking to the Wampanoags. From them he learned that among the Indians it was known as the Thing in the Fog because that's when he was most often seen. But he had only ever been seen in this part of the Island. The Indians had long ago stopped hunting here. They just let him be. They considered his presence a good omen and they let it go at that."

She sighed and sat back in the chair, her legs crossed at the ankles. "Now, that's all I know, except for what happened the other night because I'd bet anything that you saw him."

"But how could that be? How long ago did your grandfather see him? A hundred years?"

"That would be about right."

"So maybe there's more than one. A family, maybe."

"You don't look very frightened," Mrs. Parks said and the way she said it almost made me think she had been trying to frighten me and was disappointed that it hadn't worked.

"I'm not," I said. "Maybe I should be, but for now I'll just keep on the way I am." I grinned. "It looks like I'm the only one who's ever gotten that close to him."

"And you said you gave him a karate kick?"

"I did. He ignored it as if a flea had landed on him."

"And you're still not scared?"

"Why do you think he tried the window?" I asked.

"'Cause he wanted to get in?"

"He's too big to fit through the window. He'd have known that."

"Well that's a comfort," she said.

31

"Can you think of anyone who would try a thing like that?"

"I've got no enemies, if that's what you mean, Charlie. None. I live a good busy life here and my only regret is that my children are so scattered about the country. I'd like to see a lot more of my grandchildren, you know, every grandmother wants to see her grandchildren." She smiled. "But I do get to see them in the summer and maybe that's just as well because by the time Labor Day comes I'm pretty much tuckered out."

"So's everyone."

"You got that right."

"If you can think of anything strange, or something someone said that you thought was odd, would you let me know?"

She grinned. "I didn't think you'd get chased off the case."

I stood up. "They say curiosity killed the cat, but the difference is that cats can only react to what's right before them. People see things coming a long way off, if they're looking."

"Well, you just keep your eyes peeled then."

"You think he'll be back?" I said.

She nodded. "I do and I don't much like the idea."

"I'll be around," I said. "Every time the fog rolls in at night I'll be out there. You can count on it."

"You watch yourself, Charlie. I don't want anything happening to you. I'd never forgive myself."

"I'll be careful. After all, I've seen him up close and that's not something you forget. And now, after hearing your story, I'm beginning to think he means no harm."

"Don't count on that," she said. "Remember instead that my Grandfather never hunted those woods again."

On the drive home I slowly grew aware that something didn't fit. Just what didn't fit, I couldn't say. The way that works ... you get an idea about something and it won't come clear and all you can do is try to let it go and hope that it will go on banging around inside your head until it finds an explanation. But one thing seemed pretty clear. I was going out there again and again until I got a really good look at it. Like Mrs. Parks's grandfather, I was curious.

I guess most adults would think I was also foolish and maybe I was. Only time would tell.

6

Conversation With Dinner

After practice I checked the files at the *Gazette*, copied what I thought I needed, and then headed home to spend some time memorizing the play book. I was a long way from being a football player. I still didn't know how to throw a block, or make a tackle, or how to get open when the defense had me covered.

Before dinner I went into the library and got out the topographic maps of the area around Great Pond because I was planning to hike Mrs. Parks's woods.

I'd only spent time in the woods twice when I'd gone deer hunting with dad. Most of the time we hunted for ducks in the blinds he'd built here and there all over the island or we hunted in open country for pheasant.

The duck blinds are built next to water, not in the woods. You just walk in, set out your decoys, and wait for the ducks. But walking in the woods ... well, that was something different. I mean, you could get lost. As I looked over the maps, I began to feel more comfortable. I'd bring a compass and the maps and after all, this was an island. All I'd have to do was walk out to the water.

At dinner, the conversation just sort of drifted along, and then Dad looked over at me. "Tell me more about what happened at Mrs. Parks's," he said.

I told them what I knew, trying not to reveal what I had planned but I kind of made a hash of it.

"Didn't I hear that you weren't supposed to be looking into this?" Mom said.

"Sure."

"But you are," she said.

I shrugged. "Who wouldn't? I mean, it's a pretty neat story, isn't it? Some big monster lurking in the woods? They make movies about things like that. Just look what they did with sharks out here."

Dad chuckled. "So they do," he said.

For awhile we ate, nobody saying anything and then Dad got the conversation going again. "So my guess is that you're going to pull the topographic maps, grab a compass and a pair of binoculars and start traipsing through the woods around Edgartown Great Pond. Would that be about right?"

"It's a place to start."

"Mrs. Parks owns the biggest single piece of land left in Edgartown," Dad said. "A number of people have approached her but she's not selling. But why should she? Why not wait until the price goes absolutely through the roof. It's probably worth somewhere north of fifty million right now."

"What!" I nearly dropped my fork. "Fifty million?"

"Absolutely," Mom said. "We're talking waterfront on Martha's Vineyard, you know."

"I had no idea!"

"There's been a lot of talk about her land," Mom said "For a while there was a rumor about a golf course and then about raising the money so the land could be put into a trust and saved. I heard there was someone planning a subdivision full of starter castles too."

Well, I thought if anyone would know it would be Mom. She did after all run the hottest real estate company on the Island.

"Do either of you know anything about her family?"

Dad looked up, wiped his mouth and set his cloth napkin on the table. "I remember talking to Judge Henry some years ago. He seemed to be of the opinion that some in the family wanted to sell, but the others wanted to wait. There are five children, scattered all over the country. But they still come here in the summer."

"How does she afford the taxes?" I asked.

"Her grandfather, her father, and her husband were enormously successful lawyers in Boston," Dad said. "They were heavily into real estate and the story goes that they had a nose for which way development was likely to go so when it got there they held most of the land. I have no idea how much Mrs. Parks is worth, but probably well over a hundred million."

"You wouldn't know it to talk to her."

"Absolutely unassuming." Mom grinned. "And very smart. She has handled the money all these years and from what I hear it's just grown and grown."

"How do you know that?" I asked.

"Good question," Dad said, "because we don't, at least for sure. But you do hear things and sometimes from very reliable sources."

"Maybe she should hire a security service, then."

Dad laughed. "Not a chance. She's tight as a tick."

"How many people know about this?" I asked.

"I think it's pretty much an accepted fact here on the Island," Mom said.

"Only three wills, Mrs. Parks's father and mother first and then her husband's will were filed here. Wills are public information, so when her husband died, anyone curious enough to look it up, knew what Mrs. Parks was worth. It was a lot of money then and a probably a whole lot more now.

"She kept the land and house and took less in other assets to make the distribution even between Mrs. Parks and her brother Simon. It was a lot of money."

"How much?"

"She and her brother each netted about fifty million."

"Whoa ... a lot of money ..."

"Here's one thing not a lot of people know," Dad said. "She went to Radcliffe and graduated summa cum laude and was a member of Phi Beta Kappa. Then she did her masters at Harvard. The man she married, Jack Parks, was a partner in her father's law firm. He was later appointed as a justice on the State Supreme Court, just as Mrs. Parks's grandfather and father had been. It's quite a family. One of the most renowned in legal circles, though hardly anyone here remembers that now. Over time, I think she's just become old Mrs. Parks, one of our eccentric multi-millionaires."

It explained a lot, mostly the way she had of looking more into you than at you. But here was something weird. Why would a woman like that ask a high school kid to look into this for her? Why not hire some private eye from Boston? Was there something she wanted to hide and figured a kid wouldn't be sharp enough to discover it?

"How old is she?" I asked.

"I don't know exactly," Dad said. "Early eighties, maybe."

"What about the voodoo stuff?" I asked.

"I never heard anything about that," Mom said.

"There were some rumors," Dad said. He shrugged. "But about someone like Mrs. Parks, there are always rumors. What made you think of that?"

"I heard the rumors."

Dad grinned. "I wouldn't put much faith in any of that being true."

"I'm reading up on it ... just in case."

"Can't hurt," Dad said.

The thing about my conversations with my folks is that I always wind up with a whole lot to think about.

"How's the football going?" Dad asked.

"I know a lot and I don't know anything all at once."

"Think you can handle it?"

I shrugged, not because I wanted to avoid answering but because I really didn't know.

7

To The Woods

Then, for the rest of the week, there was nothing but football. On Wednesday I learned how to put on the pads and that morning, in tackling practice, I got hit for the first time. Tom Snelling did the work and he is one of the bigger guys out there. He came straight at me as I carried the ball and I side stepped just a bit at the last second so he only got me with his arms and brought me down.

Did it hurt? It's hard to describe. I can tell you that he grabbed me and held on and I hit the ground fairly hard, but I knew it was coming and it was more like falling down than getting slammed. Your body prepares itself, the muscles tightening, and you brace for the impact. The most it does is jar you.

So I just bounced up and ran back to the line. I don't

know what I had expected but feeling normal wasn't on the list. Still, I'd been hit pretty hard in karate matches and this hadn't felt all that different. I just shook it off. In a way I can't possibly explain it had even felt good.

The next four times, I pretty much escaped. Twice, I simply spun away from the tackler and though the other two times I wasn't quite quick enough, neither player got a straight shot at me so the worst part was hitting the ground.

Unless you play football, you're gonna think I'm crazy when I say this but it was pretty cool stuff.

Then the lines switched and I had to make the tackles. The coach instructed us carefully, just as he had done the others, and from the start I knew I had it in hand. I got four chances and I made all four tackles cleanly. Karate helped. I'd learned how to spot a shift in the way somebody moved when they were trying to evade you. I knew how to compensate and I nailed each one of them solidly. Size and weight figure into your ability to tackle, but so does speed. It helps to remember that nobody goes anywhere without their midsection, so that's what you watch. Shoulders, head, and feet do all the faking.

Each day I liked it better but the best parts were always when we ran the offense and I'd go flying down the field and make a cut and then another and Pete would drop the ball into my hands and I'd fly for the end zone.

Nobody could stop me and nobody could stop Charlie

41

Dollarhide either. We were both fast and both knew how to cut to get open, and once in the open we were gone.

Every day I kept a close watch on the weather, waiting for a foggy night so Pete and I could stake out the house. But we'd gotten into one of those stretches of perfect late August weather with hot days and cool clear nights.

On Saturday morning Pete and I climbed into my truck and headed for Edgartown Great Pond. I had the maps and compass and I had already studied them carefully. Mom had gotten a survey of the Parks land and I had superimposed that over the topographic map for the area so we were pretty well set.

We'd brought lunch and two large cans of tick spray because you just don't go walking on Martha's Vineyard in the woods without protecting yourself. For some reason we have the perfect climate for tick breeding. As a result there is plenty of Lyme Disease around, not to mention Ehrlichiosis. But if you go prepared, it's not a problem. Even so, when you come back out of the woods, you run a check for ticks.

We parked in a wide spot in the road and I had called Mrs. Parks on my cell phone to tell her what my truck looked like so she'd know who was parked on her road.

Man, it was a hot day, the temperature around ninety and no wind, so the damp air from the water just dripped down into the woods. It made you feel like you were walking in molasses.

What we did was follow the compass headings I had written on the map, walking from the water back to the property line and then after following the property line a way, we'd head back to the water.

We'd made two crossings and both of us were soaked through with sweat.

"Just what are we looking for?" Pete asked.

"I don't know. Something odd, something out of place, maybe some big footprints down on the beach or where there's a clearing."

"So I should be looking down and not up, then."

"Well, both really."

Pete laughed. "Yeah, right …"

We plunged ahead, pushing through the shin-high huckleberry and the vines, both of which make walking in the woods on the Island a particular chore. But it was interesting, if only for the number of deer trails we crossed and the number of times we flushed quail and pheasant and jumped deer. The property was alive with wildlife, particularly songbirds.

We'd reached the halfway point on the map when Pete stopped and wiped his forehead. "Walking through this pucker brush is tougher than practice, you know that?"

"You wanna take a break?"

"No. I wanna get it over with."

I picked up the pace some because, in truth, we weren't

finding anything even the least suspicious. And we went on finding nothing until we started a diagonal cut back toward the water and I stepped out onto a wide path.

"Whoa, what have we got here?" I said.

"I wouldn't want to jump to any conclusions," Pete said, "but it kind of looks like a path."

"I think it is."

"Yeah, definitely a path. And a pretty well worn path."

In fact it was not only worn right down to the bare ground but it had to be five feet wide. My first thought was bird watchers because the Island was crawling with them.

Pete started to turn to the right, heading down toward the pond and I stopped him.

"Let's go the other way first. We know where the path goes if we turn right."

He shrugged and followed. It was easy walking and after struggling through the woods, it was a nice break.

About a hundred yards later we stopped, looking down the trail to where it dropped into a deep swale, bounded by surprisingly steep sides, surprising because on Martha's Vineyard the ground is sand and gravel and clay and when material like that piles too high, it usually slumps downward pretty quickly. But here the walls were steep, not like a gorge where the rock walls go straight up, but steep enough, and they were covered with trees and brush.

"Let's take a look and then go back," I said.

Again Pete just shrugged.

The swale was maybe thirty feet below the surface of the surrounding terrain and we could see where the path wound down and then up the far side and off into the woods.

"This place is weird," Pete said.

"Yeah." I felt it too.

"It's like the air suddenly got heavier."

"We need to check it out," I said.

"Naw, let's go back." Pete stood with his hands shoved into his pants pockets.

"Just to the end where it goes back uphill and then we'll turn back," I said.

"Okay. But no farther."

At the bottom of the swale, suddenly I knew we were being watched. I don't for a second believe in extra sensory perception, but at the moment, in that gorge with the air so close and heavy, I had the feeling that we weren't alone. In fact, I knew it, though how I knew it, I had no idea.

I glanced from side to side without turning my head, hoping I might get a look, but if there was something there I couldn't see it, though I had no doubt that it could see me.

"This place gives me the creeps," Pete said.

"I wonder why it does that."

"Then you feel it too."

"Something," I said, " but I don't know what."

We stopped and turned back where the trail began to

climb uphill out of the swale. Both of us scanned the sides, trying to peer through the trees, mostly oak here, big sturdy oaks which, because they were down out of the steady sea winds, grew very straight.

"Who do you suppose made this path?" Pete asked.

"It must be the wildlife people or the land trust folks." I looked down at the path. "Kind of odd that there aren't any footprints, though? Weather like this, you'd think the birders would be all over the place."

"Let's go," Pete said and this time I heard an urgency in his voice which had not been there before.

"Okay."

We walked back through the swale and we had almost come to the end when something caught my eye. Movement and shadow. That's all. But it was enough.

"Don't look now but we're being watched," I said. "Just look out of the corner of your eye to the right at about one o'clock."

"I don't see anything."

"It's there. Look for movement or a shadow where there shouldn't be one."

We started up the hill. "I saw it!" Pete whispered.

"Just keep walking."

"How about we run? Running would be good here."

"No. Just walk. I don't think it knows we've seen it and we might get a better look where the woods thin out."

We didn't. But what we did see convinced us that we we'd come to the right place. Footprints. One set of absolutely huge footprints and they were imprinted right over the ones we had made coming in on the path, which meant it had been following us the entire time since we had turned onto the path and we had to assume it was following us now.

We followed Pete's advice. We ran. Fast. Very fast because the trail was smooth and it offered nearly perfect footing. We shot past the point where we had happened onto the path and kept right on running, downhill now, and we didn't stop until we broke into the clearing at Mrs. Parks.

Then we walked back and forth on the road, catching our breath.

"Well," I said, "now I feel really stupid. Before this case I never ran from anything in my life. Now I've done it twice and it's beginning to piss me off!"

Pete took a long deep breath. "I think it was the right thing to do." He bent over and leaned onto his knees. "Anything with feet that big is not something I want to tangle with, Charlie."

"Maybe it's harmless," I said.

"Big is not harmless."

"I just wish I'd gotten a better look."

"I saw all I want to see," Pete said. "Look, it's football season and I need all the sleep I can get and something like that is sure to give me nightmares."

I shrugged. I wanted him with me but if he didn't want to be part of this, I wasn't going to push him.

I looked back up the trail, searching through the trees either side, wondering just what lurked out there and whether it was dangerous. "There's a cold front coming through," I said. "Tomorrow night it'll be foggy."

"And you'll be here."

"Aren't you the least bit curious?"

"Sure. Of course I am. What kind of thing is that to say?" He stood up and shook his head. "What I don't like is that thing being curious about me."

"What makes it touchy," I said, "is that now it knows we're likely to be here."

"You sure know how to make a guy relax," Pete said.

"Some stuff I'm really good at."

He laughed. "Well, I'll give you this. You sure as shine can catch a football."

"You think I'll make the team?"

"You and Dollarhide are both starters."

"You can't be serious!"

"Hey. Guys who catch footballs the way you guys do, win football games." He grinned. "And they make quarterbacks look really good for the scouts."

8

It's All About Fishing

We drove home, picked up our rods and tackle and loaded the big wooden fish box into the bed of the truck. We stopped on the way to load ice into the box and top off my gas tank and then headed over to Chappy.

The blues were starting back with more arriving everyday. The false albacore had turned up, schools dipping in close to shore and then scooting out to deeper water. Bonito had begun to prowl as well and the bass were always around.

Even so, you can make a lot of casts, waiting for a school to show up, but hey, that's a part of fishing ... and a pretty good part too. How bad can it be? You're sitting on the beach, the weather is warm and you can even take a swim and cool off if the sun is too hot.

And if things really get slow you can go dig some

cherrystones or quahogs. It's the Vineyard. It's alive.

We drove out over East Beach, about halfway to Cape Pogue and stopped.

What few fishermen there were had pretty much scattered themselves along the beach, but very few were fishing. The tide had just started in and most always that brought fish, but the great thing about fishing is that you can never be sure. You stand on the shore looking out at all that water, nothing on the horizon but the smudge that is Nantucket, and you look at your plug and it doesn't seem possible that such a small object in so much water will ever be seen.

What keeps your faith up is that you've done it before, hauled off and fired that plug out as far as you can and had a blue absolutely hammer it.

We finished up the lunch we'd brought and rigged our rods, Pete going with a silver and blue Kastmaster that worked under water, while I chose my favorite, a pale green Spofford Ballistic Missile, a surface lure, designed to make a lot of splash and draw attention.

The waves were only medium sized, breaking very close to the shore and we stood, barefoot, in shorts and began to cast, sometimes with the tide, sometimes against it. Usually, fish will face into the current, but when a school is moving it will often come down the tide and turn if it finds the prey it seeks.

Blues are always in search of food and they are not terribly fussy. But if they don't turn up where you've decided to fish, you can either wait or move on. Just then they were employed elsewhere.

After a bit I stopped and sat on the beach, my rod butt jammed into a rod holder made of PVC. I can sit, looking out over the water for a long, long time, letting my mind drift and drift.

Most of the drifting had to do with whatever was roaming Mrs. Parks's woods and whether I had the courage to go back out there and confront it. Not that I had much choice. I wanted a good long look at something that wore shoes that big. And I could, after all, take my shotgun. I had a hunting license and that allowed me to carry the gun, though I thought perhaps it might be smart to check the hunting regulations to see whether there was anything in season I could legally claim to be hunting. Always cover your bases.

Pete drove the butt of his rod into the sand and dropped down onto the beach next to me.

"They caught 'em here yesterday," he said.

Pete goes fishing to catch fish. End of story.

"They'll be back," I said.

"I been thinking. Did we really see anything out there?"

"Something. And we sure saw the footprints."

"Anybody could make footprints," Pete said. "I saw once in a movie how a guy put on bear paws and made everybody think there was a bear around."

51

"Why would anyone do that?"

He shrugged. "To scare her?"

"Mrs. Parks."

"Well, not Madam Chang."

"No. Clearly not." I laughed. "So the next question is why would someone want to scare her?"

"Good question, isn't it?"

I pressed my lips together and made a little smacking sound several times. "Let's look at some reasons. One, she has something that somebody wants. Two, it's payback time for something she did to someone else. Three, huh … she refused to join the conservation crazies."

He laughed. "She did that?" He ran his hand over his head. "Girl's got guts."

"That's what I heard."

"Clearly a hanging offense," Pete said.

I laughed "At least here."

"Okay. Four, she, uh, help me out here, Pete."

"I don't know. Maybe she kicked somebody's dog."

I laughed and shook my head. "It would help if we knew or could figure out what this thing wants. Does he want her to move away, for example, maybe sell the land and go to live with one of her kids."

"How could we know something like that?"

"Pretty tough," I said.

"But getting her to sell the land … I think a lot of people

are interested in that."

"You remember all that talk about a golf course?" I said.

"Did you know which piece of land they were talking about?"

He shook his head. I glanced absently at the tracks of our bare feet in the wet sand down toward the water. And then it connected. The tracks we'd seen were not boot tracks. They looked like the tracks of a giant bear. So what was up with that? Were there two Things in the Fog?

Suddenly I stood up, staring hard at the water. "There are fish here," I said, grabbed my rod, and started into a cast. The Ballistic Missile splashed down and I started to reel. It hadn't gone six feet before a big blue swirled behind it, missing the plug.

I saw Pete change to a surface plug and I heard him cast and saw his plug hit the water and just then the blue took another shot at my plug and I nailed him. A few seconds later Pete hooked up.

They were good, big fish, running around ten pounds and for all the fish I've caught, blues are still my favorite. They fight with no thought of saving energy, slashing, sounding, leaping into the air. No matter how many of those fish I catch, there is no thrill to match it. My system is pumped, my heart hammering until I either lose him or land him. And when they're like that, feeding in a frenzy, slashing through the bait, you become a part of the frenzy, casting and retrieving, hooking up, seeing big swirls behind your plug when they miss and then arching your back into it when they hit it squarely and hook up.

All my plugs have the barbs on the hooks bent down so the fish I don't keep can be released and survive. But not having a barb to hold the hook in place means you have to work a whole lot harder to keep the fish from shaking off. It means you have to concentrate on keeping the line absolutely taut with not an inch of slack.

In the end it makes you a better fisherman and it gives the fish a fighting chance. They can still get free even with a barbed hook, but they're more likely to injure themselves and any injured wild animal has less chance of survival.

A pickup stopped behind us, a truck with some writing on the side and two guys climbed out wearing hats and sun glasses and headed for the water. They set up just past me, leaving plenty of room.

I was concentrating so hard on fishing that I didn't pay any attention to them until the bigger of the two, a guy about six-four started casting. He was using a fly rod and even though the breeze from the water was light, I couldn't imagine how he could get the line far enough out — until he started casting.

In seconds he had his entire line in the air and then he let it shoot out and drop and the big gaudy fly hit the water and a blue smashed into it and hooked up. Then I turned and looked and I knew right away who it was.

Everybody who lived on the Island knew Rob English. Even the guy in the trench coat and slouch hat knew him well enough to say hello to. But I wasn't sure how to react anymore. After all, he'd just finished his first summer pitching in the minor leagues, throwing four no-hitters and going twelve and 0. That pretty well set him apart. I mean, he wasn't just a guy from Martha's Vineyard High School anymore.

I guessed the other guy, the one fishing with a surf rig and also casting a Ballistic Missile, and who was, by then, playing a fish, was his older brother, Carl.

I landed my fish, cut his throat, carried him to the truck, and dropped him into the fish box, then rushed down to make a second cast. Now the whole school seemed to surface at the same time and it was one mighty school. Bunkers, chased by the blues, came shooting out into the air and the blues came right out into the air to grab them.

Then the gulls appeared, coming over from Cape Pogue Pond which lay directly behind us. It was wild! It was everything blue fishing is supposed to be and then WHAM! I was into another fish.

The blues had a large school of menhaden trapped against the shore and they hammered into them mercilessly, cutting some of them in half. What floated to the surface, the gulls got, or other blues swallowed.

Other fishermen showed up and by the time I'd caught four fish there must have been fifty guys throwing plugs.

Only Rob English had a fly rod. But probably not too many people could have handled a fly rod in a situation like that with a breeze blowing directly onto the shore.

And then … it stopped. The water lay smooth and the gulls picked up the remains of the menhaden, which we call bunkers. Both schools had moved on.

But it had been the stuff that blue fishermen live for and everywhere men were laughing and talking and they had broken out the beer as they cleaned their fish and tucked them safely onto ice.

"I've been hearing about you guys," a voice said from behind me as I dropped my last fish into the box. Everyone of them was right at about ten pounds. A banner day.

I looked around, stuck out my hand, and smiled.

"Hey, Rob, how's it goin'?"

"Everything's good," he said as we shook hands.

"I never saw anyone throw a fly that far," I said. "Forget about the wind."

"Let me see if I've got this right," Rob said. "You and the big guy here, along with another guy named Dollarhide, aren't gonna lose a game this season."

I laughed, trying to be at least reasonably modest, but that sort of stuff never occurs to Pete.

"Nobody can stop us," Pete said as they shook hands.

Rob grinned. "Stay cocky," he said. "It works."

"We've been hearing about your season," I said. "Triple

A next year?"

Rob nodded. "I've already signed the contract."

"That is awesome," I said. Then I grinned. "I only wish I was as certain as Pete about this fall."

Rob's brother joined us, carrying a beer for himself and a soda for Rob. "Can I get you guys something?" he asked.

"Thanks," I said, "We've got a cooler full … of soda."

It's the thing about the Island. We were all out there on East Beach fishing and when you've got a thing like that in common it's like you'd all known each other all your lives.

Other men began to drift over, all of them shaking hands with Rob and Carl and talking about what a great season he'd had and how he was gonna be in the majors by the middle of next season. And they talked to Pete too, because he was the best quarterback the Island had ever produced.

What seemed even more improbable was that the two best athletes ever from the Island were standing there talking. I gotta tell you, it was awesome.

I got to watch and listen and for the first time I heard something I had never heard before: grown men, adult males praising guys our age for ability. Of course, most of them still didn't know that I was playing football, but all of them, it turned out, had heard the story about how Pete and I had cleaned the clocks of those hoods out in Menemsha. I told you, once the summer people leave, it's a small town.

For me it was enough to watch and listen.

And then Pete slapped me on the shoulder. "The reason we're gonna take the state championship this year is this guy right here. Charlie Jones. This guy's got the best hands I ever saw and he runs the forty in four-seven."

"Don't forget Dollarhide," I said. "He runs it in four-o."

"I've got two wide receivers that can get open, catch the ball, and fly. And this guy here runs right through tacklers. It's gonna be wild."

And just like that I was part of something so big that it absolutely boggled my mind.

Out of the corner of my eye I saw Rob raise his head and turn toward the water, even as I caught the scent on the breeze. Both of us grabbed our rods and headed for the water without saying a word. The fish were back. Nobody believes me, but I know I can smell them. Later, Rob told me he can smell them too. How cool was that, me sharing something with Rob English? Get out of here ...

By the time the fish had gone and we were wrapping up, the sky in the west had turned, as the old timers say, sort of smurry, gray and foggy above the water, and in the shifting breeze you could smell the change in the weather. A cold front. And now, with the water still warm that meant fog ...

9

Bigger than Big

The front came through like a train with great rushing winds and rain so heavy it flooded the streets. And then it passed and pushed on out to sea. In an hour the temperature dropped twenty degrees and the fog rolled in.

Around eight I called Pete.

"You going with me?"

"I can't," he said.

"What's up?"

"Family night."

"Uh-oh. Your parents on another guilt trip?"

"You got it."

"Hey, it happens." I sighed.

"They just get all caught up in what they're doing and suddenly decide they need to pay more attention to us."

"Better that way than the other."

"Pain in the butt, but I think you're right."

"It's cool."

"Are you gonna go anyway?"

"Yup."

"You got guts, Charlie, I'll give you that."

"It's nothing like that, Pete. I just get curious."

"As long as it doesn't get in the way of football."

I grinned. "Not likely."

"This is pretty weird, Charlie."

I changed the subject. "Don't I remember that your parents know Mrs. Parks, and your father worked for them when he was a kid. See what you can get them to tell you about the family and whether they all got along."

"Sounds like you smell a rat."

"Just opening doors, that's all. Sooner or later we'll get enough of them open and then what now seems absolutely crazy will be understandable."

"Like the big-footed thing in the fog."

"Sure. All this stuff has an answer somewhere. We just have to know where to look."

"I'll see what I can get. And hey, when you get back, call me on my cell, will you."

"You worried?"

"Of course I'm worried. You're my ticket to a division one school, man."

I laughed. "Now there's a rare thought."

I left the truck well down the road from the house and threaded my way on a long diagonal down to the water and then up toward the house. I was dressed once again in fog gray and I wore a gray anorak to keep the dampness off and to provide some extra warmth because the temperature was in the low fifties.

I stopped at the water and looked off into the fog, wondering again if this was truly such a good idea. I might be a black belt and a boxer and an athlete, but the truth is, big wins, and all this guy had to do was hit me once.

The stuff you see in the movies where some 110 pound girl who knows karate beats up some six-four thug, weighing about 230 pounds, is a lot of crap. To take someone you have to hit them hard enough to hurt them and the bigger the guy is, the more punishment he can absorb. End of story. Except for this — you wanna be strong — you work at it.

But despite all the skills I'd been working on, there was one I didn't have. I needed to be a hunter, a stalker who could find his prey and track it over any sort of terrain. But I couldn't begin to do that, and knowing I couldn't had begun to cut into my confidence. It was a new experience.

I wondered if it weren't smarter to just turn back and let the police handle it. The trouble was that they weren't handling anything. I knew from what Dad had said that Chief

Espinoza regarded Mrs. Parks as something of a screwball. And, in truth, over the years, he'd gone out on a lot of calls from women who were living alone. In psychology they call that a generalized reaction. Because experience has taught you one thing, you apply the idea to everything else and that blinds you to the one fact that is, in fact, different.

And Mrs. Parks was different ... very different. In the first place she was smart, and I had the feeling that not much frightened her. What's more, she'd been living alone for ten months out of each year for a long, long time. She simply was not the sort to panic. And, in fact, she had not panicked. She had very quietly asked for my help.

That raised a question I still could not answer. Why me? Why a kid? Why not hire some big time detective from Boston? How had she even known about me?

What those thoughts produced was the conviction that I had to stay on the job. Mrs. Parks was counting on me and the one thing you don't do is let people down. And anyway, all I had to do was watch.

The key lay in understanding what posed a threat and what was only show, because the way I saw it, what had happened so far was just for show. There was something else going on. There had to be, if only because there always is.

I started up the slope from the water, avoiding the wide stone path from the house because even in the fog I'd be easy to spot in the open.

It helped that the woods here had been manicured. There was no underbrush and the fallen limbs had been cleared away. It was like a park and I could slip silently from tree to tree. The fog helped in another way too. It had soaked the ground making it soft underfoot and very quiet.

Each time I stopped, I listened, waiting at least three minutes before moving closer to the house. Just below the brow of the hill I stopped again and looked up into the trees. The glow from the house surprised me because of its size and I assumed Mrs. Parks must have turned on every inside and outside light. Well, why wouldn't she? Who wouldn't with something like that hanging around outside?

I eased up over the brow of the hill and stopped, concealed by the fog and trees. Now, I could see people moving around inside. Several people. One large shape did most of the moving, drifting back and forth in the big living room behind the gauzelike drapes that covered the broad atrium doors, a restless shadow, but from the herky-jerky sort of movements and the abrupt starts and stops, I knew that whoever it was, he was angry and arguing with the others in the room. He was also very tall and very broad.

The mind, always a tricky devil, especially my hyper-imaginative collection of cells, leaped to the conclusion that it must be one of her sons. The family ran to large people, the men well over six feet and the women just under.

But no matter how logical his presence there seemed, I

wanted evidence. What I needed to do was get closer. I needed to get right up against the building so I could maybe hear what was being said. I assumed from the body language that the man would be shouting, or at least speaking loudly enough for me to hear.

I gave a quick thought to motion sensitive lights I couldn't see in the glare from the floodlights, but if I came in from the blind end of the house by the barn I could reach the wall of the building and avoid the sensors ... if there were any.

And if the Thing was out there ... well, he was out there, and if he saw me it was simply the risk I had to take because I needed to know what was being said.

I kept low, using the fog to hide me, but staying well back into the woods until I reached the barn and then, picking a dark path between the lights, I ran for the house and plastered my back against the silvery weathered shingles.

I waited, I stared out into the fog, but the lights, refracted by the water droplets suspended in the air, made it impossible to see into the woods, or even past the edge of the lawn.

Down along the wall I went, keeping below the windows and stopping when I reached the atrium doors that led to the terrace.

I never got to hear a single word because huddled down against the wall, about fifteen feet away at the other side of those doors was a great hulk. I'd come up so quickly and, I assume, because he had been listening to the talk inside and hadn't been paying attention, that I had taken him absolutely by surprise.

He simply stood up and his head reached well above those doors which were one full step below the level of the terrace and he was well over a yard wide. All I could see was his silhouette and then he moved away, fading into the fog like some sort of ghost.

My heart was pumping so hard I could hardly swallow. I let him go. The fog made it impossible, or at least it provided a good excuse not to get myself hammered. Instead, I walked around to the front of the house, took a deep breath, and rang the door bell.

The big man opened the door. I'd taken my head cover off and I grinned.

"Hi. Charlie Jones. Mrs. Parks asked me to keep a watch for her?"

He said nothing. Just stared and I gotta tell you he had what I would call a significant stare, his eyes narrowed, shooting out diamond-like glints. He pretty much filled the doorway and he was not fat. He was just huge, with enormous biceps and pecs and delts, and a neck like a tree trunk.

He turned his head and called into the house. "Mama? You know anyone named Charlie Jones?"

"You let him in here, Walter," she said. "He's the only one who believes me!"

He smiled and seemed to relax. And then he offered his

hand. "Sorry if I seemed a little confrontational," he said. "I guess you know things are a little uneasy around here these days."

I smiled back and my hand almost disappeared into what was more like a clamshell bucket on a crane.

But my hands are pretty large too and in his smile he acknowledged the strength I put into my grip.

"It's okay," I said. "Everyone's a little out of sorts just now."

I followed him into the living room where two women and another huge guy rose to greet me. Mrs. Parks did not get up, but in weather like this I knew her arthritis was probably chewing away at her joints.

"Now," she said, "this is Charlie Jones. He lives down in Edgartown and I asked him to help me here. You already met Walter and this here is James and these beautiful ladies are their wives, Jessica and Eleanor."

I nodded and said hello and shook hands with them. It was a big room but these people made it seem tiny. Both women were over six feet and the men hovered right about six-seven. Made me feel like a shrimp.

"Now everybody sit down," Mrs. Parks said and then she turned to me. "What brings you here tonight, Charlie?"

"The fog. He seems to like the fog. It's easier to move without being seen."

She smiled. "Did you see him?"

"Just before I rang the bell." I pointed to the doors. "He was huddled down just outside there and I surprised him." I pointed to the right side of the doors. "And then he stood up and walked off into the fog. There was no point in chasing him. Even if I caught him I couldn't have done anything. He's way, way too big."

"How big is that?" Walter asked.

"Pretty close to eight feet." From their expressions it was clear they didn't believe me. "He was standing on the ground about a foot below the level of the sills and his head reached above the top of the doors and that adds up to just about eight feet, maybe a little more."

James smiled. "Is there anything you can show us?"

I got up and walked to the doors and swung them into the room. "Out here. You can see his tracks." I took out my super powerful tactical light and when they stepped outside I shone it down onto the tracks. It was impressive.

"My God," Jessica said. "He's got feet even bigger than yours, Walter!"

"Damn," James said. "What are those? Size twenty five or maybe thirty?"

The women stepped quickly back inside and the men followed and I closed the doors.

Walter shook his head. "He makes Shaq look like a dwarf. Even Yao."

"So maybe I'm not going senile after all," Mrs. Parks said.

Both men looked at their mother and shook their heads. Finally Walter spoke.

"Well, it settles one thing, Mama. You can't stay here alone. You're gonna have to come home with one of us until this gets sorted out."

"You know what it is, don't you?" Mrs. Parks asked.

James smiled. "The old legend from grandfather."

"Of course." Mrs. Parks smiled.

Suddenly I was aware that both James and Walter were staring at me.

"You're a pretty brave guy," Walter said. "You knew how big he is and yet you came out in the fog and took him by surprise. Now why would you do a thing like that?"

"Mrs. Parks asked me to."

Walter turned toward his mother. "How did you pick this fella out?"

She grinned at him and then at me. "You been away too long. You got no idea what goes on here anymore. Last summer that young man and a friend of his, Pete Heyward, beat up four professional hit men out in Menemsha. One of 'em wound up dead and the other three are in jail waiting to be tried because there were warrants out on them. And on top of that there's a story that Charlie and Pete outfoxed a pack of government spooks from some secret agency." She looked around at me. "There any truth in that, Charlie?"

I nodded but I said nothing. There are times when it's

best to be modest.

"And now I hear through the rumor mill that he's the greatest wide receiver we ever had here and his friend Pete is the best quarterback we ever had here and they got another kid, a part Indian from Aquinnah, can run like the wind." She looked around at me. "I heard he did the forty in four flat. Is that right?"

"Charlie Dollarhide," I said. "Last spring he set the state record in the hundred meter as a freshman. And he can cut and fake and he's got terrific soft hands."

Walter and James both laughed. "Mama, you always did love football."

"I never miss a home game. Can't travel the way I used to, but I never miss a home game."

With the conversation relaxed and easy, I decided it was time to find out what they had been talking about and sometimes a direct question at the right time gets an answer. But even so I was a little nervous. After all, James and Walter Parks had both been huge NBA stars in their day, and I knew they saw me as a kid. How could they not? I was.

What I did was take the plunge.

"When I came up on the house from below I could see someone pacing back and forth and it looked like a pretty hot conversation was going on. What were you talking about?"

I saw their mouths drop and then Walter laughed. "You

don't hold back, do you, Mr. Jones?"

I grinned back at him. "Something's going on and I need every bit of information I can get. Right now, I'm pretty much in the dark."

I could see that I'd stirred the pot and I could also see that they weren't used to having a kid ask questions like that. But if it bothered them, it didn't bother Mrs. Parks.

"They want me to leave my house. 'Course, that was when they thought I was going senile and having visions of monsters as a result of living by myself. Well, they'd know better if they saw me at the bridge table."

"Mama," James said, "we're only thinking about your safety."

"Well, I suppose that's so," she said. "But I'm not inclined to leave this house awhile yet. Not 'till I have to, I expect."

"You could hire some security," I said. "So far all he's done is try to get a window open. But even if he had, he couldn't have fit through the opening. What's more, he picked a small window instead of the big one three feet away."

"So," James said, "the inference is that he's sending some sort of message. And if that's so, and Mama doesn't take the hint, then the next question is whether he'll escalate his behavior in order to make sure she does what he wants?"

I nodded. "That's what I'd expect."

"Mama?" James said.

"I'm staying. You want to get some security people, I got no objection."

It was time to leave. "I've got to get home," I said. "It was nice to have met you all and I hope to see you again."

Walter walked me to the door.

"Are you still planning to keep watch?" he asked.

"I won't need to if you get some security people here." I looked down at the floor and then way back up. "Probably be a good idea to tell them not to shoot. They're probably not carrying enough firepower to do anything more than get him mad and if he attacks they haven't got a chance."

Walter nodded. "We'll let you know what we decide," he said. Then he smiled and offered his hand. "Thanks for being here when Mama asked. Nobody else wanted to listen to an old lady. And that makes me wonder why you did."

"She asked me. I knew she wasn't making it up."

He clapped me on the shoulder. "I think maybe I'll see one of those football games this fall."

"That'd be awesome," I said.

I walked out to the road and then stopped. Once again I could feel his presence. It was almost like he was talking to me without making any sound. It took everything I had not to run.

The other thing was that the footprints had looked different, more human, except there seemed to be some sort of claws on the toes. But no boots. Definitely no boots.

10

Another Case

I'd just finished changing and sat down to read the stuff from the *Gazette*, when my cell phone rang.

"Hello?"

"Hi, it's Mandy."

"Hi," I said.

"Listen, there's something I need to talk to you about. Can you come over?"

"Sure. Be about ten minutes."

She'd sounded worried, maybe even a little scared. And what I didn't need just now was some new little mystery. I had enough on my plate, though I was pretty certain I was about to have a whole lot more.

She opened the door and smiled. "Come on in." She led me into a large room to the right of the front hall, the room that, when this big old Captain's house was built, would have been the front parlor that nobody used except when the minister came to call or somebody died.

Now it was a library and her parents were sitting there reading.

"Mom, Dad, this is Charlie Jones."

They both stood up and we shook hands. I knew them by sight but I'd never been introduced before. As always I gave them my best sir and ma'am greetings. Good manners always works with parents.

"So," Mr. Bunce said, "I hear we have a championship football team this year."

"Got the best quarterback in the state, guys who can catch what he throws and a whole lot of other guys who can make it happen."

"That's what I heard."

"We'll know when we play a game," I said. How weird was that, I thought. I didn't even know for sure that I'd made the team. All I had was Pete's word.

"Well, good luck," Mr. Bunce said and I followed Mandy out to the kitchen.

She crossed to the refrigerator. "Coke okay?"

"Coke's great." Now, right here, you have to know I was on new territory. I hadn't had anything to do with girls since I was about seven and I had never been alone with a girl in her house, and well, I was nervous. Maybe even terrified.

We sat at the table in the center of the room.

"What's up?" I asked.

"Well, maybe it's nothing, but I heard how you are really good at investigating things and Charlotte King said that the other night, when she got out of work at Mad Martha's, someone followed her home."

"She's sure she was followed? I mean, there are a lot of people on the streets now."

"She said he followed her all the way to her street and when she turned he stopped and leaned against a tree until she went into her house. When she looked out from upstairs, he was gone."

"Can she describe him?"

"About your height, but skinny. He has thick dark hair, long, tied in a pony tail and maybe a large tattoo on his right arm. He was wearing jeans and a white tee shirt and black running shoes."

"Did she tell anyone?"

"Her parents and her boss. Her Dad's gonna walk her home."

"How close did he get?"

"She didn't say."

I slid down in my chair, resting my arms on the table.

"Have they gone to the police?"

"No."

"Which means they aren't sure how serious it is."

"What do you think?" Mandy asked.

"Serious."

"Will you check it out?"

"What time does she get out of work?"

"Ten."

"Okay, I'll have a look."

"Won't he see you?"

I shook my head. "Not a chance."

The look I got back was brimming with questions of the kind I don't like to answer. Nobody believes I can do what I say. I mean, how does a guy my age learn to follow people so that they don't know they're being followed? Well, first you read all the books you can find and then you practice. I'd spent the past two summers practicing. I'd pick someone out of the crowd, day or night, and tail them. After awhile I got pretty good at it. Of course, the people I tailed had no reason to suspect that anyone was watching them. This guy would be wary. Just how wary he was would tell me a lot.

If the guy was a psycho, then once he saw Charlotte's father with her, he'd know he'd been spotted and he'd be looking for a trap.

With her father there I doubted he'd try anything, and what I wanted was to follow him back to where he was staying. Then I'd be able to identify him and turn the case over to the police. Maybe he had a record.

"When will you start?"

"Tomorrow night unless it's still foggy. Then I've got something else to do."

I finished my Coke and pushed back in my chair.

"Will you tell me what happens?"

"Is she working tonight?"

"No. Tomorrow."

I nodded.

"Thanks for your help, Charlie?"

"Sure," I said. "See you at school?"

"Of course."

11

Practice

Monday the heat and humidity returned and even the stretching and warm-ups seemed like work. I could tell that a lot of the guys hadn't done much over the summer or even since last football season because they were stiff and sore from last week and you could see it in the way they moved.

But the first stringers were all in good shape. They knew the drill. You want to play well, you work and work and then you work some more. You focus on your goal. There is only one goal. Winning. Anyone who thinks otherwise is either a loser or a fool or both.

Coaches like to win. The guys who can help them win get to play. Winning is why we play the game, it's why we keep score. Anybody who thinks differently is an alien from some distant planet sent here to weaken the population so they can take us over without our ever knowing.

On Monday, wearing full pads, despite the heat, we went to work and it was awesome. I guess I knew by then that I'd made the team, because I was playing on Pete's squad and so was Charlie Dollarhide. And there was one other sophomore, a tight end, Jon Nelson, and he was big and quick and he knew the playbook. He also liked to hit and he hit hard.

He also understood pass protection, and how to block for the run and he could catch a pass too. The pass protection was critical because Pete is a pure drop-back passer. Not that he couldn't scramble to avoid a tackle, or even run if he had to, but his style was to take five steps back, then one up into the pocket formed by his offensive line. Then he threw.

Like any drop-back passer, he depended on his offensive line. They held off the defense and gave him time to find his receivers downfield. Football is absolutely a team sport. Every player has to do his job or it doesn't work, even if you've got the best running backs, receivers, and quarterback.

Those guys can't do anything if the linemen don't open the holes for the backs, or protect the quarterback. Just watch the Patriots. You'll see everything you need to know about how a team should work.

We've also got a really strong defense, with three big, fast linebackers and a decent secondary. But to match up with our passing game they'd had to have been the best secondary in the state. We smoked 'em.

Coach posted the list showing who had made the team before lunch break and my name was there. It's hard to describe just how that felt. I mean, I was sure I'd made the team, but seeing my name on that list was the biggest rush I'd ever felt.

After lunch it was hard to get my helmet on.

Pete and I rode home in my truck and he was pumped. The offense was working. The pass plays worked, the running plays worked, and because we'd played havoc with our own defense, it was clear that other teams were not gonna find it easy going.

He couldn't stop talking and instead of dropping him at his house we went back to my house and the pool house I used as my office. When we moved into the Waters's old house, I'd convert the small garage out back into an office.

I got us both sodas and we sat and finished coming down from a football high.

"So," he said, "what's up with the monster?"

"I saw him again."

"You did!"

"Pete, this guy is close to eight feet tall and I'm gonna guess maybe 400 pounds."

He whistled softly. "That's the size of a bear."

"It's not a bear. It's human." I ran a hand through my hair, still slightly damp from the shower. "Or maybe sort of human."

He laughed. "Hey, it's either human or it isn't."

"There are stories," I said.

"What kind of stories?"

"From long ago. I'm gonna ask C.D. if he knows some-one in the tribe I can talk to. I looked up some stuff in old newspapers. Knowledge is power."

"Muscles are power."

"One kind," I said, "but maybe not the best."

"Until you need 'em."

He had me there. It was why I'd worked so hard at ka-rate and boxing and pumping iron and running. A P.I. has to be tough because he always deals with the unexpected.

"In any case," I said, "what I know now is that over the years there have been many sightings of some sort of huge, hairy creature on the Island, all of them in the same area. No one was ever harmed. But I gather it kept a lot of people out of the woods. This has been going on since before the En-glish got here." I finished my soda.

"The thing is it runs in fits and starts. Sometimes fifty or sixty years went by without a single sighting and then sud-denly there would be a rash of them."

"Like now."

"Maybe. So far I'm the only one who's seen him."

"Does this thing have a name?"

"The Algonquins called it a sasquatch. In other places

they're called a bigfoot or a yeti. They've been seen all over the world. Some tribes believed they were protectors and it was a good omen to see one. Most everyone else was just plain scared."

"I take it you're not," Pete said.

"He's done nothing to make me think he's going to attack. In fact, just the opposite. He runs away."

He stood up and walked to fridge. "You want one?"

"Sure."

He brought back two icy-cold Cokes. "Charlie, I'm not sure what to make of this."

"Neither am I." I grinned. "But I got to meet James and Walter Parks."

"Whoa ... now that's cool."

"You can't believe how big they are close up."

"How'd that happen?"

I told him they wanted Mrs. Parks to stay with one of them for awhile and also how she refused. "They're bringing in some security people from Boston."

"So that lets you out, right?"

"It worries me. I'm afraid they'll start shooting."

"Maybe they'll get him."

I shook my head. "All they'll do is piss him off and then things could get really dangerous."

"What about the voodoo?"

"I don't know what to make of that, if anything."

"You're like a magnet, you know that?" Pete said. "You draw in all sorts of really weird stuff. I mean, why don't you get some simple thing like a murder to work on?"

"Got something else too." I told him what Mandy had told me about the stalker, and what I planned to do.

"Now that's something I could help out with," he said.

"He'd spot you in a second."

"Who says?" He looked hurt, his lips drawn into a pout.

"Me. I've spent the last three years learning how to follow people without them spotting me. I even had Dad go for a walk and I told him I'd be tailing him. He never saw me and I don't think he believed I had even been there, until I gave him a list of where he'd gone."

"Well, suppose you set me up along the way and we jump the guy and pound him so he gets the idea?"

"If nothing else works we may do that."

"Yeah!" He smacked his fist into the palm of his hand. "He'd spend the rest of his life looking over his shoulder. We could wear hoods so he didn't recognize us."

Pete likes extreme behavior. But one of the things I'd learned in football practice is that if you're gonna be good, then you push yourself to the extreme. There's no other way.

"I'll let you know on this one."

"I'm ready."

What I didn't say was that if the guy was a rapist he most likely carried some sort of weapon and there was no sense taking that risk unless we absolutely had no choice.

12

Things To Be Said (*by Pete*)

Okay, here's my two cents worth. I was gonna write more, like I did the last time, but the thing is I'm way too busy with football and doing all my homework, which is something I never did before. And then too there's all the stuff I have to do for Charlie to get ready for the SAT's, especially now, because of the new test.

He's got me doing something called Spuzzles, and reading novels with special vocabulary words … man, it's like walking in harbor mud on the low tide. But I'm doing it. I don't have any choice.

But all that aside, some things need to be said. Here's the first thing. He's a Division One ball player. He doesn't know that but when I was at football camp earlier in the summer I saw a lot of receivers and maybe one or two had the speed and power Charlie has. I mean defensive secondary guys hit him and bounce off. And he understands the little things that separate the good guys from the great guys.

He never uses the same fake twice and that's why he gets open. The other Charlie, C.D., does it with pure speed. Charlie Jones makes the defense think one thing and then he goes past them. Not many Division 1-A guys will catch him when he gets into the open.

But he doesn't know that. He didn't even believe he'd made the team until the list went up. What's with that, huh?

Even now, now that's he not only made the team but is going to start, he never stops trying to get better and once you understand that, it's like a disease. I thought I was pretty well up to speed, but watching Charlie I began to think about what I did and I found ways to get better. He's infected the whole team. He hardly ever says a word but everybody knows. Coach knows.

We were a winning team before Charlie came on, but now we're a championship team.

On the other hand, I'm feeling pretty guilty about not helping him out with this monster (or whatever it is). Sure, I went out into the woods with him, but not many guys have the courage to go slinking around in the fog at night.

But there's something else too and this is big, in fact it's even a little scary. The night after Charlie told me about Char-lotte, I went for ice cream at Mad Martha's, and I made sure a bunch of the guys from the team were there and we all got our cones and kind of clustered around out on the sidewalk. I know that wasn't what Charlie wanted but I have a thing about some guy threatening kids and I figured maybe we could pick him off and teach him about our rules.

We hung around till Mad Martha's closed and Mr. King met Charlotte as she came out. We all said hello and laughed like there was nothing going on, and we let them get a head start before we kind of meandered along well behind like we weren't going anywhere special, you know, just a bunch of guys hanging out. I think there were maybe ten of us.

The farther we got from the center of town the fewer people we saw and I slowed us down. We were laughing and talking and having a pretty good time all in all, but hard as I looked I never saw a sign of anyone following the Kings. So a couple of streets before theirs we turned off and wandered back to the center.

Not till the next day did I find out what happened and by then the whole Island was talking about nothing else.

It turned out that some guy had come out of the dark pointing a gun at Charlotte and her father. The way the story went, he threatened to shoot Mr. King but another guy, nobody knew who, had come out of the dark and taken the gun from the guy and pretty much trashed him. Put him in the hospital, in fact.

That's all I knew, except that I was pretty darn sure who

the second guy was and I cornered him in the locker room when the other guys had left for the field.

"Is it true?" I asked him.

"Is what true?" He was lacing up his cleats.

"That you took out the guy who attacked Charlotte and her father."

He sighed. And then nodded. "I saw him pull the gun and I moved up to where I could get to him so that if he pulled the trigger the bullet wouldn't hit anyone."

"And?"

He grinned at me. "I took him out."

"And into the hospital …"

"I lost it, Pete," he said. "The guy is a total slime bag and he has a record of assault. Rape. The cops think maybe he's connected to a series of rapes and murders in Toledo, Ohio. Same description. Same M.O."

"M.O.?"

"*Modus operandi.* The way he operates."

"What'd you use on him? Karate?"

"Just to take the gun away and then I went to boxing. You wanna hurt someone you box. Short, hard punches from the top of your shoulder with everything you got into them." He shook his head. "I got carried away. I think it was the thought of what he had intended to do. It was like I could see into his mind. It's a good thing Mr. King stopped me. I'm pretty sure I was gonna kill him."

"Damn … you are one nasty guy! Who would have guessed, huh?"

"Not me," Charlie said. He finished tying his left shoe and stood up.

"You okay now?" I asked.

"Sure. Fine. But it took me a long while to calm down last night. Hours." He shook his head. "I never knew that I could lose it like that. It's a good thing to know."

"What's gonna happen to the guy?"

"They're running some DNA tests and if they get a match he goes back to Toledo to face murder charges. Eight of them. But I don't need any DNA match. I saw into his mind last night. They got the right guy."

We left the locker room and trotted toward the field.

"And by the way," Charlie said, "it's good you guys turned off when you did. Somebody would have got shot."

"I never saw anyone following the Kings," I said.

"He was there. But he's done this a lot and he's very good." He grinned. "Just not good enough. He never knew I was there. And another thing. Don't tell anyone it was me who took him out. Just let it go the way it is."

"Don't the Kings know?"

"I was wearing a ninja hood."

"But why wouldn't you want people to know?"

"Pete, let's just say it's better this way."

It left me with a lot to think about. I mean, try this. Most of us think we're pretty brave and in fact, I think most guys are when they have to be. But what Charlie did goes way, way beyond brave and I was pretty sure I didn't know anyone who could have pulled that off. Sure, I held my own with the hoods in Menemsha, but that was different.

This was cold and calculated and he'd made every move just right. What's more he could do it again and again just the way he did on the football field. And what I wanted more than anything was that we'd both go to the same college and get to play together for four years. And I knew where I wanted to go. UConn. They had the coach I wanted to play for: Randy Edsall. I decided to call and let them know about Charlie Jones. I'd already talked to them during the summer and I knew a scholarship offer was coming as soon as the NCAA rules would let them make an offer.

Still, one thing about what Charlie said worried me a lot more than I wanted to think about. It was the part about seeing into the guy's mind. Did he really do that? Could anyone do a thing like that? I made a note to ask him if he could see into the mind of the monster or the sasquatch or whatever he called it.

It could make you nervous hanging with a guy who could read what you were thinking.

13

On The Carpet

I was sitting in my office, thinking about college and which ones I would apply to. I'd had a list for a long time, which included Dartmouth and Harvard, Bowdoin and Williams, but football had changed some things. It probably meant that with my grades and my SAT scores, and if I had the season Pete kept telling me I was gonna have, I could get into all of them.

But it also raised some questions. Was I good enough to play Division One? Look, I can be as stupid as the next guy about some things and one of them is sports. Sure, I'd done the research and I knew that running a 4.7 forty was big time. My size helped. So, suppose I had a really outstanding year. Would I qualify?

I kept spinning that idea around and around in my head,

trying to find a place where it fit, but there didn't seem to be an appropriate slot. Maybe I just wasn't used to dreams of that size.

Then the door opened and in walked Dad with Chief Espinoza, and they brought the smell of trouble with them.

"Hi," I said, trying to keep it light, but both of them looked as if they'd eaten a lot of raw onions at lunch and still hadn't digested them.

"Charlie," Dad said, "I'd like to hear your side of what happened last night." They both pulled chairs up to the desk. I have a lot of chairs in my office. It isn't clear why. I don't have many clients.

But one thing was clear. I had to tell them. I don't lie, as a rule, and this was certainly one time when I wasn't even going to try an evasion. Still, I wondered how they knew.

"What do you want to know?"

"Everything," Bart said. He sounded unhappy.

"Mandy Bunce told me that a guy had followed Charlotte home and I set up to tail him. When he pulled a gun I had to move in and stop him."

"But you did a little more than that," the chief said.

"I lost it."

"Lost it?" Dad said. "Charlie, you almost killed him!"

I wouldn't lie, but I wasn't backing down either. "Did the DNA check out?"

The chief shook his head. "How did you know about

that?"

I shrugged. "Just a guess."

"Why would you guess that?"

"Because he was too good at following someone and that meant he'd had a lot of practice. Pete and a bunch of the guys from the team had followed the Kings for a way, but Pete never saw anyone so they turned off."

"But you suspected something even before you followed him," Bart said.

"I checked the web. I looked for stalkers and unsolved rape cases and the guy from Toledo turned up."

Bart shook his head. "That's really good police work, Charlie."

"Thanks."

"But there is the question of the beating you administered," Bart said.

"I told you, I lost it. I knew what he intended to do. He was going to shoot Mr. King, rape Charlotte, and strangle her. It made me sort of ... angry."

"The trouble is, Charlie," Dad said, "that a thing like that can cause problems for the prosecution. The defense might make the claim that the police beat him and that raises a red herring that could get in the way of a conviction."

"I'm not a lawyer, Dad. What I did was take out a really bad bad guy and for some reason I thought nobody knew who had done it."

"Some people suspected," the chief said. "I couldn't think of anyone else on the Island who could have done that by himself."

"You know, I don't think I did anything wrong here, but I'm starting to feel like I'm some kind of criminal."

"Why didn't you go to Bart?" Dad said.

I didn't want to answer that question. I knew it would piss Bart off, but there wasn't a whole lot of choice. "Because when I've gone to him before, nothing happened. Like the problem Mrs. Parks is having." I looked right at him. "Have you done anything about that?"

"Com'on, Charlie, you know Mrs. Parks. She's an old woman living alone. She hears all kinds of strange things."

"Well, she heard this one all right and I've seen what she heard twice." I grinned. "Didn't Walt Fears tell you about this?"

"He made his report," the chief said.

"And you didn't believe us."

"It's pretty farfetched," the chief said.

"I know what I saw," I said.

"Just what did you see, Charlie?" Dad asked.

"Whatever it is, and it hardly even seems human, is eight feet tall and probably weighs about four hundred pounds. The last time I saw it her sons James and Walter were there and they saw the footprints. Now they're hiring security guards."

"How did you get into this?" Dad asked.

"Mrs. Parks asked me to."

Chief Espinoza scratched his head. "But why would she ask you?"

"You mean, why would she ask a kid?"

"How well do you know her?" Dad asked.

"I used to see her at the library a lot and I guess she was impressed with what I was reading. She's really smart and she recommended some books and we talked about those and then after I got my license I used to drive out there and we'd talk about books. And then too, she heard about what happened in Menemsha last summer."

The chief shook his head. "I guess I better go talk to her."

"Now wait a minute," Dad said. "You actually saw this this ... whatever it is?"

"It's probably a sasquatch," I said. "They've been seen in that area for a long time. It goes back to the Tribe, long before white men came here."

"With the security guys there, you had probably better stay clear," the chief said.

"I told them to make sure not to shoot. But I know they're gonna shoot and who knows what that will mean?" I folded my arms over my chest and let my chair tip back. "The first time I saw him I hit him with the best kick I could muster and it just bounced off. I don't think he even felt it."

Dad grinned at Chief Espinoza. "Looks like you've got a

real hummer of a mystery."

"And no time. Well, Labor Day's almost here and then things'll calm down for awhile."

"If it's a sasquatch," I said, "I don't think it means any harm. But I still don't know why it's started turning up. The Indians saw it as a kind of protector. They never hunted there. Mrs. Park's grandfather hunted until he saw it and then he quit. He only hunted ducks after that … at least here."

The chief smiled and sat back in his chair. "I'm thinking I ought to find some money in my budget and hire you as a consultant. You sure do have a way of getting information."

"I like information," I said. "You can never have enough."

"The problem," Dad said, "is making sure you have it right before you act."

"What should I have done, Dad? Should I have taken the gun away from him and then held him till the police got there? I could've, I suppose, maybe that's what I should have done. And maybe I would have if he hadn't thrown a punch at me after I knocked the gun away. Last summer with the hoods in Menemsha, it was different. I didn't even know who they were. But this time … this time I let it all hang out."

"Coach tells me," the chief said, "you're the toughest guy he ever coached. He says guys just bounce off you."

"That's a trick. I never give them a solid target. You learn that in karate."

"Okay," the chief said, "here's the thing. You can't do

that again. This guy has a broken jaw, busted nose, broken cheekbone, along with a whole bunch of ribs. He looks like he was run through a meat grinder. You just can't do that sort of thing, Charlie."

It pissed me off. We were talking about a bad guy and I was getting the lecture. "He had a gun," I said. "I was unarmed."

And suddenly, Dad was on my side. "Is it wrong to subdue a dangerous criminal?" he asked.

The chief's eyebrows shot up and then he grinned and shook his head. "Absolutely not. I'm only trying to say that Charlie lost his cool this time. He has to be very careful. He has to keep himself under control."

"Fair enough," Dad said and then he looked around at me. "That okay with you?"

I nodded. "I didn't know that about myself. Now I do. It's a good thing to know."

14

Another Walk In The Woods

The next morning it rained and we worked in the weight room and ran some passing drills in the gym. I was surprised to find out how many guys had never worked with weights, and both coaches spent a lot of time explaining and showing them the exercises they needed, not only to bulk up but to prevent injury.

The key to that is leg strength. But then, in sports, everything starts with the legs.

Pete and I went to my house for lunch, and then Pete went home to work on another book of spuzzles and I headed for the woods. The rain was warm and I wore a rain parka and rain pants over my shorts and tee, and Bean's rubbers to keep my feet dry.

This time I came in from the other direction, parking on

a piece of land that belonged to one of the conservation groups and then heading down a well-used path and into the woods.

Here and there other paths diverged to one side or the other, and they were blazed so you could follow them without getting lost. I had a compass with me and the topographic maps in a plastic pouch in my pocket.

Not that I was worried about getting lost. Hey, it's an island. You can't get lost on an island, especially on the Vineyard. You might not know where you are at any given time, but you can't get lost unless you panic and start walking in circles. But when you have a compass there's just no way you get lost.

I walked perhaps a mile or two on the path until I reached an open barway in the stone wall. I stopped and pulled out the maps and knelt down so I could shield them from the steady drizzle with my parka.

I found where the conservation land ended at the wall. The next piece, some fifty-two acres, more or less, belonged to somebody named Tifton.

On a gray rainy day bright colors show distinctly and looking either way down the wall I spotted long lines of orange surveyor's ribbons. From what Mom said, people only surveyed their land when they were getting ready to sell, or after they had bought the land and were planning to subdivide, which required a Class A survey.

It turned out that it was an oddly shaped tract, very long and narrow, in places no more than fifty yards across. On the far side the land belonged to Mrs. Parks.

It took me awhile but I walked the entire boundary of the Tifton piece and at the northerly end I found more survey markers on a piece of land belonging to somebody named Kresky. It was only twenty acres, but the map showed that it had frontage on South Road. It also bordered Mrs. Park's land.

That meant access. I might not be in the real estate business, but I'd listened to the conversations at home. You pick up a lot if you listen, but to be honest here, I enjoyed knowing about things like that. After all, on the Vineyard, real estate is a major topic of conversation, if only because land is limited and incredibly expensive.

I looked at the topographic map, oriented the map to the south, using the compass, and located the ravine on the map. South southwest.

I put everything away and using the compass began navigating a direct line … well as direct as I could. I wasn't worried about the security people. They'd be in by the house and the ravine was a long way from there. Besides, those were almost certainly city guys and they'd stay out of the woods.

I hadn't gone but a hundred yards when I could feel him. He was somewhere off to my left and keeping pace with me, but in the misting rain and the cover offered by the trees I couldn't see him.

But he was there, and I know this is gonna sound crazy, but I had this strange feeling that he was protecting me. There was a way to test that, of course. He would know about the guards. What would happen if I headed for the house? Was it worth the risk?

I shook my head. No. I'd go to the ravine and then take the big trail back out to my car.

However, now I took my time. I wanted to see him, to get close to him, to know what in the devil he was. All that, of course, was up to him.

I made it easy enough for him to know where I was. Not intentionally. I told you I hadn't spent much time in the woods and as a result I kept snapping twigs and my rain pants made all sorts of noise as they rubbed against the pucker brush.

Rain gear is not the best thing for walking. You sweat and the moisture can't escape. I had better rain gear, Goretex stuff that was supposed to breath, but I had decided not to risk tearing it in the woods. So I sweated as I walked, stopping now and then and holding my breath, the better to hear, but all I got was silence.

I kept checking the compass, looking ahead, lining up on a tree and walking to that before taking another sighting. It worked perfectly and I walked right to the edge of the ravine and stood at the top, looking down at the wide trail and waiting.

Finally, I sat down on a big rock and waited some more. You do a lot of waiting in the detective business, and sometimes it pays off.

Suddenly he was there, on the other side of the ravine, looking directly at me. I could easily make out his eyes and now I could see the rest of his face and it was covered with nearly black hair. But he wore clothes, and that set me back some. Why would he wear clothes? Where would he even find clothes that size? It wasn't like he could walk into a store and order up a pair of size seventy-two jeans, at least not without causing a pretty major sensation.

All he did was look at me, but as he did, I began to feel a new sensation and it was absolutely malevolent. What I had felt before was gone. I stood up and began the walk around the ridge to the road, checking back over my shoulder. He stayed where he was, watching me retreat, but he made no move to follow.

When I hit the trail I took off. Even running in rubbers I fairly flew over the smooth surface, only stopping when I was sure I had run far enough and fast enough to have some margin of safety.

My wind came back quickly as I walked rapidly along and then I stopped dead, looking down at the ground.

There were his tracks, clear in the damp surface of the

trail. But the stunner was that there was a second set of tracks, easily the size of the boot marks, only these tracks were like the ones I had seen at Mrs. Parks's house. They were rounded and indistinct except at the toes where the claw prints showed perfectly as they curved down into the damp ground.

I had no idea what it meant because my head was pretty much of a muddle. I think for the first time in my life I felt the edge of panic. What I wanted to do more than anything was run. So instead I took a long deep breath and walked along at a moderate pace.

Then I turned, walked back to the tracks and with my foot rubbed out the tracks with the claw marks. Don't ask me why. I had no idea. I just did it. Call it instinct. Call it crazy. Sometimes I do things like that. I don't know why I do them. I can't explain it.

A short while later I passed through the barway and onto conservation land. I knew by then that I was alone. I also knew I had a whole lot of thinking ahead of me and I needed to talk to Pete. I needed to see what someone else thought.

And ... I also needed to talk to Mom ... about real estate and who had bought the Tifton land as well as the other piece. Clearly, something was in the works.

For a while, I don't know how long, I sat in my truck looking off into the woods, thinking about what I had just seen.

I thought about Occam's Razor, the idea that the best solution is often the simplest solution.

Based on that, the footprints I had seen meant there were two things loose in the woods. But one of them wore shoes and clothes and the other did not. And clearly the one with claws on its toes had been following the one wearing boots or shoes.

I thought back to when I had rubbed out the clawed tracks. What had I understood without understanding what I had done? Questions like that can make you crazy.

Consider this. On the football field when I needed to throw a fake to get past a defender, I never thought about what I would do. I just did it. Instinct. Pure instinct. But instinct conditioned by my karate and boxing training. I acted on some set of visual signals I picked up from the player opposing me and for now, that worked.

Still, knowing that I could react instinctively, got me no closer to understanding why I had wiped out the one set of tracks and not the other.

See? Make you crazy.

15

Discussion At Dinner

That night, about halfway through dinner, having listened to a lot of warnings about what a dangerous guy I was and how I needed to exercise control and how I needed to forget about being a private eye and let the police handle things, I decided that I was tired of being made to sound as if I had done something wrong.

Had to be careful, though. If I exploded it would only make their point about my "dangerous temper" and that would lead to greater control.

I took it slowly. You do that by asking questions. "Mom," I said. "What was I supposed to do? Let the guy shoot Mr. King, rape Charlotte, and then kill her too?"

"The point is what you did to that man."

"I think the point is that I stopped him." Then I drew

from history. "How many times have I heard you say about some murderer you read about in the paper that somebody ought to be shot, because going to prison wasn't enough?"

"Those were just words."

It was working. She was on the defensive. "If I hadn't been there, two people would be dead and he'd have been off-Island before the bodies were even found. He had a moped hidden in the bushes."

"Charlie," she said, "the thing is, you can't get into stuff like this! It's simply too dangerous!"

Well, of course a mother is going to think that way. And it had been dangerous. If I'd missed his gun hand, he might have shot me. That's why I have a black belt. Karate is first about defense.

"Dear," Dad said, "you're right. Charlie should not have lost his temper, but to be honest, I think this is a guy thing. In the same position I think I might have killed the guy. Bart says he would simply have shot him once he saw the gun. It also looks like the guy is a serial killer, wanted in Toledo." He looked around at me. "What's hard is to adjust to the fact that my son is capable of handling himself so well."

"This is more than that!" Mom said.

"It is," I said, "but I knew what he was going to do."

"How could you know that?" Mom was incredulous.

"Because it was like I could see into his mind and I not only wanted to stop what he was about to do, but to make sure he didn't survive to do it again. After all, at that point, at the point when I took the gun away from him, all he could have been charged with was illegal possession of a firearm and attempted robbery."

"You're right," Dad said, "but it still would have kept him in jail for several years."

"You can't see into someone's mind," Mom said.

"I just knew."

"When will they get the results of the DNA test?" Mom asked.

"A week or so, I should think," Dad said.

Dealing with parents is a constant negotiation. You have to give up something to protect whatever freedom you need. So, in the end, I agreed that I had gone too far. Then I changed the subject before I had to agree to something else.

"Mom, what's going on with the Tifton property?"

Took her by surprise, I can tell you. She spit out a mouthful of peas and the little green buggers went rolling all over the table and the floor.

"Oh!" she squeaked. "Look at what I've done!"

We all got busy picking up the peas and then before she could take a mouthful of the mashed potatoes, which would have been nastier to clean up, I asked the same question.

"It was bought by Greenlands, Incorporated."

"A developer?" I asked.

"That's what they do," she said.

"Did they buy the Kresky piece too?"

"Why do you want to know this?" she asked.

Dad sat quietly, working his way through the food on his plate, but missing nothing. He is a lawyer, after all.

"Because it borders Mrs. Parks's land."

"Uh-oh, here we go again."

"Nobody wants to help her, Mom."

"So that leaves it up to you?"

"Well, yeah, I think it does."

"Why would she do that? Why would she ask you instead of the police."

"She did ask the police," I said. "They ignored her."

"That's crazy. That's their job!"

"You know," Dad said, "crazy old lady syndrome."

"She is not exactly a crazy old lady," Mom said, "in fact, she is far and away the best bridge player on the Island. If she asks for help, then there's a reason. Have you ever talked to her?" she asked Dad.

"Can't say as I have."

"There's not a single subject she doesn't know something about. Her mind is razor sharp, despite her age."

With the conversation drifting, I brought it back to ground zero. "Could her trouble be connected to Greenlands?"

"I don't see why."

"Do you know the guys from Greenlands?"

"I sold them both pieces of land and Dad closed for

them."

"Uh-oh," I said.

"Why is there suddenly an uh-oh?" Dad said.

"Now I've got to deal with a conflict of interest."

"I don't see ..." Mom looked over at me.

"I'm working for Mrs. Parks."

"What am I missing here?" Mom said.

"I think somebody is trying to scare Mrs. Parks into selling her land," I said.

"What?" Dad's eyebrows shot upward. It's an impressive move, because he's got really bushy eyebrows.

I wiped my mouth with my napkin. "There's been rumors for a year about a new golf course and housing development somewhere in Edgartown and a deal like that requires a lot of land. The pieces they bought aren't big enough. Nor are they all that desirable."

"How do you know that?" Dad asked.

"I walked the land this afternoon."

"In the rain?" Mom looked startled, but then she had never liked going out in the rain. Parents are hard to explain.

"I had my rain gear on and most of the time it just drizzled. It was an easy walk because of the survey markers. But in places it's very narrow. What they need is Mrs. Parks's land and she has no intention of selling."

"I have no idea how you figured all that out," Mom said, "but the people at Greenlands told me they're planning to make her an offer she can't refuse."

"They didn't run a Dunn and Bradstreet on her then."

It was Dad's turn to be surprised. But he tried to come at me from the side. "And what would that show?"

I grinned and he grinned back, knowing I'd bagged him. "Like you said, she's got a ton of money. And because of her family I suspect she's got a lot of clout up in Boston."

"More than you can imagine," Dad said. "When you've had three State Supreme Court justices in the family, people tend to listen. And the money doesn't hurt either."

"This whole thing is making me really angry," Mom said. "I think those guys, instead of going through me, are going to her on their own so they can cut me out of a commission. I think they just made a really nasty enemy."

"So … not a conflict of interest then."

They both laughed. "In fact, a united front," Dad said.

"It's comforting," I said.

"You want to tell Mom the rest?" Dad said.

"In the fog, at night, and only in the fog this thing turns up outside the house. It's about eight feet tall and weighs maybe four hundred pounds. I've seen it twice."

"Good God! You can't be serious!"

"Yeah, Mom, I am."

"What is it?"

"Well, the only thing it can be is a sasquatch." I told her the rest of what I'd seen, but somehow I skipped over the part about the two sets of tracks. I don't think I intended to, but I did, and later I thought maybe it was because I wasn't sure of what they meant. So we left it there. I also forgot to tell them about the clothes it wore. Hey, you can't remember everything.

On Tuesday school opened. That took seven hours a day and football took another two. But Labor Day had taken most of the summer people with it and traffic dropped and people walked on the sidewalks again. It would get busy when the Fishing Derby got rolling but that came later. Just then all I could think about was Saturday and our first game. I was so high I felt like I was walking on my toes.

Pete saw that, of course, and he kept trying to get me to calm down. He was right. You never play well when you're too pumped up. You have to find a middle ground.

So Friday night I put in an hour hitting the big bag and the speed bag. It's the best kind of exercise. You have to focus. Later I went through several sets of Tai Chi, which always calms me down. It worked. I slept like a stone.

But in the morning I shot up out of bed like a rocket. Game Day! It was my first and there is no feeling like it.

16

Game Day

The morning disappeared in a haze that had nothing to do with the weather. My head kept whirling and my thoughts refused to follow any sort of logical line. But then, as I looked around, I realized that every one of my teammates seemed to be pretty much off the walls too.

Except Pete. He was Mr. Cool, calm, and collected. But this was his turf. This was what he did and he had done it for an entire season the fall before. But so had a bunch of the other guys and they were all as tizzified (if there is such a word) as I felt.

But then we ran out onto the field and began warming up. It helped. What did not help was the crowd. And while it wasn't exactly Fenway, it seemed like it to me. After all, I'd spent a lot of time in the background, staying out of sight, keeping below the radar, and suddenly I was on stage and a wide receiver has nowhere to hide like the guys in the line.

You're out there, in the open, and if you drop the ball … well, I tried not to think about that.

Bourne kicked off, and Caleb Strong fielded the kick and ran it back about fifteen yards so we wound up on our forty yard line. Not everybody plays either offense or defense because there just aren't enough good athletes in a school of our size. But I only played offense as did Pete and C. D.

We trotted out onto the field, went into the huddle, and Pete called my number. I'd been hoping I could sort of ease into things. I thought maybe he'd call a running play and all I would have to do was block downfield. Not old Pete. He believed in initiation by fire.

I was set wide right and on the snap I ran at the defensive guy in front of me, twitched my shoulders to the right and when he corrected to keep with me, I went past him like he was standing still and I was in the open and I looked back as the pass from Pete fell into my hands, catching me perfectly in stride and then I cut in my afterburners.

I had only the free safety to beat and he was a lot smaller but he had a good angle, meaning no matter how fast I ran he could cut me off before I got to the goal line.

I put my head down and motored, waiting for him to get close enough to try a tackle, knowing his only shot was to take my legs out. I saw him start to lunge and I jumped. High.

Like I was a hurdler. I hadn't even known I could do that. Talk about instinct. Who knew? He slid past beneath me and I coasted the last five yards into the end zone.

The place was an absolute madhouse and my teammates were pounding me on the shoulders and knocking helmets as I trotted off the field.

As I stood there, watching us kick the extra point and then setting up and kicking off, I was a pretty happy guy. They say everyone gets about five minutes of fame. And I thought if I never got to experience it again, I'd be okay with that. But I didn't believe it. I wanted more. I wanted all I could get.

The Bourne guys were pretty much discombobulated. The touchdown on the first play of the game had rattled them and their timing was off. Two running plays went nowhere. They tried a pass play and the quarterback threw behind his receiver and it fell to the ground incomplete.

We got the ball back on the punt and ended up at about our thirty-five.

Then, in the huddle, Pete called my number again, only this time it was a double crossing pattern in the middle where C.D. and I cross. I go shallow and he goes deep.

My defensive guy was ready and he didn't fall for the outside fake, so I went outside, got him committed and then spun to the inside and I was open. To be fair, he didn't have much time to make his decision. In fact, he had a half-step and then I was past him, and I just plucked the ball out of the air and turned upfield.

But now I had three guys to beat and then I saw C.D. cut back my way and I drew the defense, getting them to cluster, and at the last second I turned and flipped the ball back to C.D. We'd done that in practice a couple of times, just kind of fooling around because Coach wasn't big on that razzle-dazzle sort of stuff.

I've told you C.D. can run, but he was totally pumped and his legs were an absolute blur. Besides there was nobody ahead of him, so he opened up and showed everyone why he'd broken the state record in the hundred meter.

Well, if it was nuts before, now it was pandemonium. Just like that. Two plays and we were up fourteen-zip.

We had demoralized the other team. It's the way you win. You make the other team believe that they can't beat you.

But after that the game sort of settled down. Bourne managed to gain some yards on the ground, mostly with their big fullback. It took four guys to bring him down.

They got a couple of first downs and then coach had our middle linebacker, Bosco Baines, key on their fullback and he made a couple of really hard tackles and they had to kick.

Then we went to the running game. On those plays C.D. would go short and turn to the outside to draw their outside linebacker away from the line and I ran a slant in, so the middle linebacker had to cover me.

And Caleb showed why he was our running back. But he also had Jon blocking for him and man, could he open his end of the line. Caleb carried us to two first downs and then on the third series, they adjusted and on a third and four, Pete called C.D.'s number on a post pattern.

I had to use a lot of fakes to get open before I could draw the free safety in to help cover me. C.D. just ran and Pete uncorked a forty yard toss that dropped into C.D's hands as he crossed the goal line. I don't care how many football games you watch, you'll almost never see a better pass.

Well, I'm not gonna take you through the whole game. Bourne finally scored a touchdown in the fourth quarter when we had a lot of subs in the game but all it did was keep them from being shut out. We won fifty-six to seven and that is pretty much a blowout.

In the locker room, before we hit the showers, Coach spent nearly a half-hour trying to get our swelled heads back to normal. We knew what he was doing. We knew he was right. But we wanted praise. Heap it on! Give me all you got! I can't hear enough!

The shower room was a madhouse, guys shouting and singing and snapping towels, and I showered and got out of there before I got hurt. Those guys were like a bunch of Neanderthals surrounding a fresh kill.

I dried off, put my clothes on, and dropped down on the bench next to C.D.

"I need a little help," I said.

"With what?"

"I need to know about old Indian legends on the Island. Do you know someone I can talk to?"

Now C.D. might be a sophomore, but he steps down to no one. Why should he? He's as tough a guy as there is here and yet, he's got this quiet way about him.

"What kind of legends?"

"Older the better."

"The guy you want is Pete Smith. He's been collecting those stories all his life."

"Can you introduce me?"

He grinned. "No introduction needed, Charlie. He was watching the game. Just call him up. He's in the book. Besides, everybody on the Island knows who you are after this summer."

I shook my head. "It's no good having a reputation."

He grinned. "Cuts down on the bullying."

"I suppose it does."

"But let me ask you why you don't want to introduce me to Mr. Smith?"

"Easy enough. You've got a reputation and after what happened to our family last spring, I have to keep a low profile. And after what happened with the Kings, you are kind of outta my loop."

"What about the Kings?"

"Com'on, Charlie. You might not have owned up but everybody knows it was you because there's no one else on the Island who could have done that. And besides the guy was wearing a black ninja suit.

I shook my head. "Not good," I said. "But listen, you never heard me admit to anything, right?"

He laughed. "Sure. Never heard you say anything one way or another."

"Yeah, that's good."

"Rumor has it you're onto something else too. Got anything to do with Indian legend?"

"Maybe. I don't know for sure yet."

"Well, tell Mrs. Parks I said hello."

Well, that one knocked my socks off. "How do you know about that?"

"Dad built all the cabinets when she redid the house this summer. I went along and helped. He was there last week to make some adjustments."

"Might be good not to noise that about either," I said.

"Okay with me. Heck, I never talk to anybody anyway."

"You sure I can just call Mr. Smith?"

"Use my name if you want."

"It's a good name," I said.

"It is now." He grinned. "Kind of iffy there for awhile."

17

Hanging Out

I hadn't been in my office five minutes when Pete showed up. He flopped into a big old easy chair, the kind that invites flopping.

"Some game, huh?" He was smiling from ear to ear.

"Think we can do it again?"

"Every time. Coach says that from what he knows there's no team in our league that can even come close."

"Yeah, but no coach in the league knew anything about me or C.D., either."

"Meaning?"

"Any one of those teams could have had a ringer move into town and we wouldn't know till we played them."

"Good point. Really good point. It means we'll have to work harder. Especially the defense."

"Best place to start."

"Yeah, I'll talk to Coach."

"That's what team captains do. They talk to the coach."

He got up and walked over to the fridge. "You want something?"

"Diet Coke."

"Diet?"

"No fat, Pete. Gotta stay lean and mean."

He laughed. "You'd just sweat it off at practice."

"High protein, no sugar."

"Yeah, lots of protein in this." He handed me the can and flopped back into the chair. "Where'd you go? I called a couple of times and left messages for you."

"C.D. arranged for me to talk to Mr. Smith about old Wampanoag legends."

"Whoa ... what have we here?"

"You know what a sasquatch is?"

"Not a glimmer."

I told him and he sat upright in the chair, his eyes wide. "Was that the shadow in the woods?"

"I think so." I shook my head. I'd forgotten about that. It was four times, not three, and twice I had felt him there, a week ago Sunday and the time with Pete.

"Man, I wish I'd known that."

"What difference would it have made?"

"I wouldn't have been there."

I laughed. "There's nothing to worry about, Pete."

"Easy for you to say. Me, I get bad dreams from watching a scary movie. And this is football season and I need all the sleep I can get."

"I'd really like to see him close up."

"You're losing it, Jones, you're absolutely losing it."

"Nothing new in that," I said.

"I also heard you were over at Mandy's."

I laughed. "She told me about the guy who was following Charlotte."

He grinned. "I'm thinking maybe the old bachelor has finally got himself a girlfriend."

"Piss off!" I said and that made it worse. I'd shown him a weak spot.

"Soooo, then ... will we be double-dating anytime soon?"

I laughed and shook my head. What I know about girls you could put in a hermit crab's shell.

"Who does? No guy I know. You just hang around and pretty soon they talk to you and if you like 'em you ask 'em out. Nothing to it. They don't even expect you to say anything. All you have to do is grunt and smile."

"I get something on my mind, I talk about it."

"No. Bad idea. Don't say anything. Just grunt and smile. You say too much, especially anything that requires thinking, and you scare 'em off. All you do is act like you're listening and nod and smile and think about playing ball or something."

"I can see I've been studying the wrong sort of stuff."

"You just listen to ol' Pete. I'll get you on the right side."

I grinned and nodded ... up. It was a start.

Pete grinned. He'd caught it and he nodded back, moving his head up.

I set my soda can on the desk. "I'm going out there. You wanna come?"

"Nope. I'm having nothing to do with large hairy things that sneak through the woods."

"It is safe, you know."

"I'm not taking any chances."

"What am I hearing here? Pete Heyward, the guy who jumped a bunch of gun-toting thugs is afraid of the woods?"

"It's what's in the woods, Charlie. Those guys were human. People don't scare me."

"Here's the deal. There are two of them, and one of them is human. He wears clothes. A sasquatch wears hair."

"This is the eight foot tall thingy we're talking about, right?"

"Yeah."

He sat up in the chair. "You're saying there's some eight foot tall guy walking around in the woods. Where does he live? How did he get here? Anybody that tall kind of sticks out in a crowd, you know."

"In the first place anybody can get on or off island by

boat. And if there were someone working with him, and that seems pretty likely, they could pick him up and take him to somewhere private and then bring him back when it was dark, and particularly, when it was foggy."

"But why?"

"I've got absolutely no proof, but I'm pretty sure they're trying to scare Mrs. Parks into selling her land. Greenfields has bought two pieces of land that abut her land and remember all the rumors about a golf course?"

"What do you suppose that land is worth?"

"Dad says fifty million and Mom agrees."

Pete whistled and shook his head. "Pretty soon ordinary people won't be able to live here."

"Getting closer to that everyday."

Pete finished his soda. "So how do you go about proving that they're behind it?"

"I haven't worked out the details yet."

"When are you shoving off?"

"Soon."

"Okay if I hang out here and play some games?"

I grinned. Nobody loved video games more than Pete. He was absolutely addicted to them. "That's cool," I said. "I'll let my folks know you're here."

"Great! I need a break from all the studying."

"Yeah, right ..."

"Hey, I'm working. I never worked so hard. I was a little

dubious at first and then I thought about how you not only have to get into college but you have to stay there and the more I learned now, the easier that would be."

"Absolutely true. And the more you have to learn in a given amount of time, the better you get at learning."

When he doesn't get something, Pete gets this kind of blank look on his face until the wheels in his head start turning. This time the wheels never moved.

"It's called learning how to study."

"How did you figure that out?"

"I take a lot of AP courses. There's a lot of work and to get it done you have to get efficient"

"Man, you are so far ahead of me here. Do the other kids who get good grades think like that?"

"Sure. Some do. But it's their thing, right? I mean most of them don't play sports, and they have to have something they're good at. Everyone does."

"Okay, okay. I'll only spend an hour here."

I grinned. He wouldn't spend an hour, he'd spend two. And probably I could count on his being there when I got back. It's human nature. Pleasure first.

18

Getting Things Straight

But instead of just walking off into the woods I drove up the drive and stopped at the house. The first thing I noticed, simply because it was impossible not to notice, was that there were no security people around.

I walked up to the door and rang the bell and I was about to ring it again when Mrs. Parks opened the door.

"Well, look who's here! Come on in, Charlie."

I stepped into the house and closed the door behind me. "How are you?" I asked.

"Why is everyone concerned with how I am? Must be my age." She laughed and when she laughed you smiled just because she sounded happy.

"I meant, has anything more been going on?"

"Come on, let's go out to the kitchen. I'm brewing some

tea. Would you like some?"

"No, thanks," I said.

"A soda then?"

"Soda'd be great, thanks."

We sat in a corner of the kitchen by the ceiling to floor windows that looked down over mowed fields toward Great Pond. It was an absolutely spectacular view.

"Well, to answer your question, nothing at all has happened."

"What about the security guards?"

"Humpf! Some security guards. They decided they wouldn't work nights. Said it was too lonely out here and they kept hearing things in the woods. Deer, I told them, but they would have none of it. The head of the company called and apologized."

"Did you try anyone else?"

"I decided to take care of myself. I got out one of my father's shotguns, went to the store and got some double-ought buck and loaded it up. At night, I keep it by my side. In this family you grew up knowing how to shoot. I sat in a lot of cold duck blinds but I learned."

"Have you heard anything from Greenfields?"

She looked sideways at me and then slowly smiled. "So, you found out about that, then."

"My mother handled the sales on the two adjoining pieces of property."

"Does she know they tried to cut her out by dealing with me directly?"

"She figured it out."

"Well, I sent those scamps running. Told 'em I'd never sell this land. That I was born here and I intended to die here and they would have a good long wait because people in my family live a long, long time."

"Must have looked a little disappointed."

"Well, more than that, I'm afraid. In fact they looked pretty nasty."

"I think it'd be a good idea to have some people around," I said.

"You think they'll try to kill me?"

"It's possible."

For awhile she just looked down toward the water and then she sighed. "It might work," she said.

"The family would sell?"

"They'd probably hold onto the house and some frontage on the pond. The problem is that the boys play golf. They might be tempted to bargain free memberships."

"Would they do that, I mean, knowing how you feel?"

"Charlie, one of the many troubles with growing old is knowing that the things that are most precious to *you*, are not necessarily precious to anyone else. They haven't lived here since they went off to private school. For a long time, neither did I. We lived in Newton and they were raised there.

My husband had to be near Boston. And that was fine. But I took them down here every summer. I was raised the same way. We've really only ever been summer people, until my husband and I retired here. We had some wonderful years together. But the boys have grown away from it. They have their own lives, and though they bring the grandchildren every summer it's only for a few weeks at a time." She smiled. "Oh, how I treasure those weeks!"

I decided not to tell her what I had begun to believe, if only because it's not a good idea to build anything on guesses.

"I'll be checking in from time to time," I said. "Just let me know if you hire any more security. Sometimes people like that get too itchy."

She looked around at me, a question clear in her eyes. "You're going so soon?"

"I've got some people to see."

She smiled. "You don't give up, do you?"

"I want to find out just what is going on here." I rubbed the back of my neck, always a bad sign. That particular itch doesn't turn up unless I'm worrying about something and clearly I was worried. "If I find out anything, I'll let you know right away. One thing more. Can I have phone numbers where I can reach your sons? Just in case I need to?"

"You really *do* think something is going to happen, don't you?"

I rubbed the back of my neck. "Pretty sure. But it might

be nothing. I just think it'd be best to be on the safe side."

"You think I should leave and go live with one of the boys for awhile."

"It couldn't hurt. I just hate to think of you here, alone, with some thug ready to attack. I mean, it sounds farfetched, but ..."

"Maybe I'm listening. Maybe I am. Somehow, I don't think you worry very easily."

I smiled. "It's just a hunch."

"Hummmm, well, maybe it's a hunch I want to listen to. I don't know."

"If you decide to go, why don't you leave me a key to the house. Then I can check it every day."

She stood up slowly, letting the stiffness in her joints fade enough to allow her to walk. She crossed the kitchen, opened a drawer and took out a key. "Here," she said. "I think it's a good idea if you have a key, whatever I decide. It works on all the doors."

I dropped it into my pocket.

"I'd hate to miss the rest of the football season," she said. "Never have we had such a team. And that Charlie Dollarhide! I never thought anyone could run that fast."

"C.D. is incredible," I said.

"And then there's Charlie Jones. People hit him and bounce off. And he always catches the pass."

"That's Pete's fault," I said. "He puts it right into my

hands every time."

She smiled and laughed. "I did seem to notice something like that."

Pete was still at my office, of course, just as I had expected. And he was deep into another video game ... NFL football. What else? "You had a call," he said. "Number's on the pad.

I knew the number.

"Mrs. Parks?"

"I'm leaving," she said. "The driver will be here shortly. He's taking me to the airport. I've got a plane waiting for me. I'll be going to Arizona where Walter lives. You've got the numbers."

"Did something else happen?"

"You got me thinking, that's all. And then I remembered one of the men who came with Mr. Eddy from Greenfields. He was big and nasty looking. I sat enough times in court to know what *he* does for a living. Thank you, Charlie. If you hadn't come down here today, I might not have remembered that. I hope I'll see you soon."

"I'll let you know what happens," I said.

"Listen here. Don't you go taking any risks, you understand. If something happened to you on account of me I should die a very unhappy woman."

"No," I said. "I won't."

"The shotgun is in my bedroom closet. It's in a leather harness hanging from the clothes pole, hidden among some dresses."

"I'll remember," I said.

"You take care, Charlie."

"I will, Mrs. Parks. I'll be very careful. And enjoy your stay in Arizona."

"I'm sure I will. Nothing like grandchildren to keep an old woman busy."

"She's leaving?" Pete asked as I hung up the phone.

"Yup."

"That's a good thing, right?"

"It is."

"And that probably puts an end to it."

"I don't know."

"But you're not talking."

"Pete, I got a lot of things to think about here and I gotta go see someone. I just hope he's around."

He shut down the game and turned off the equipment. "You gonna need backup?"

"Not yet. But it may come to that."

"We're talking bad guys here, right?"

"I think we are."

"How bad?"

"I don't know yet, but I'm guessing about like the guys who tried to take us out in Menemsha."

"So. Really nasty guys, then."

"Not yet." I shook my head. "It might come to that."

"What're the odds?"

"Can't say yet."

"Which means they don't know about you. I mean, like they don't know you're a threat."

"But they will."

"That's who you're gonna see this afternoon?"

"Yeah."

And then, as always, Pete came through. "Hey, Charlie? Forget about football. You need help, I'm here, okay?"

I smiled. "I needed to know that."

He grinned. "As long as we're talking humans, you can count me in. And if it comes down to it, well, you can count me in on the other thing too."

"You're the man, Pete, you are absolutely the man!"

19

Meeting The Enemy

The Greenfields Development office was in Vineyard Haven at the five corners, and I pulled in, wondering if anyone would be there late on a Sunday afternoon.

They were, in fact, open and I walked up to the receptionist's desk and using all the self-control I could summon ... she was, after all, absolutely beautiful, with long blond hair and deep blue eyes and from what I could tell, because she was sitting down, had all the right equipment that girls and young women spend time showing off.

"Hello," I said, "I'm Charles Oliver Jones and I'd like to speak with Mr. Eddy, if he's in."

She smiled, one of those older girl smiles that they offer to younger guys when they think you've said something cute.

It made me feel like a little kid. But I smiled.

"What's this about?" she asked.

"Land."

"Can you be a little more specific? Mr. Eddy is pretty busy and ..."

"Land on Edgartown Great Pond."

The smile disappeared and that told me a whole lot of what I needed to know.

She picked up the phone and pushed one of the buttons. "A Mr. Jones to see you, sir," she said. "Yes, it's about land on Great Pond."

She pointed to a door. "You can go right in," she said.

So I did. I guess I should have been nervous, or scared or edgy or something along those lines. But I wasn't. I was on a mission and I was focused and that tends to make me calm.

Mr. Eddy looked surprised when a kid walked into his office and once again I got that tolerant sort of smile that you get from adults.

But I walked up to the desk and stuck out my hand. "Mr. Eddy, I'm Charles Oliver Jones."

"Jack Eddy," he said. He was about my height, but kind of soft and pudgy and he tried to give me the big power handshake but he just wasn't strong enough to pull it off. Instead he got the worst of it and it pretty much took him by surprise. Hey, I spent years walking around squeezing tennis balls to build up my grip.

"What can I do for you, Mr. Jones?"

I sat down in the chair opposite his desk and in the window I caught the reflection of a big man, still only my height, but from his size he'd spent a lot of time in the weight room and he'd sucked down more than a few steroid cocktails.

"I've been working for Mrs. Parks and she's pretty upset with you trying to buy her land. It's been in the family for three generations and it's her home."

"What gave you the idea that we're trying to buy her land?" Mr. Eddy said. His eyes had narrowed and I could tell he was trying to figure out just what was going on here. No adult can get used to the idea of dealing with someone my age on a level playing field. They're supposed to have the advantage.

I pointed to the wall behind him and the architectural rendering of the golf course and where the houses would be placed.

"Oh no," he said. "That has nothing to do with the Parks land."

"Then why does the legend at the bottom identify the land as belonging to her?"

He frowned and took a deep breath. "Look, kid, this is way over your head. We're in the development business and the way we work is we target a piece of property and then settle on a price."

"Even if they don't want to sell?"

133

"Everybody sells. It's a matter of price." He grinned, "In the end, money talks."

"I think," I said, "that may not be the case this time. She doesn't want to sell. "

"We've only just begun negotiating."

"I'm only trying to save you a lot of trouble," I said. "And I'm also trying to save her from worrying. She's an old lady."

"You know, you're beginning to irritate me."

"I'm sorry about that, I didn't mean to. I told you, I'm just trying to help." I stood.

"It's none of your business, kid."

I looked around at him and grinned. "What do you know about Mrs. Parks and her family?"

"It doesn't make any difference."

"Did you know her grandfather, her father, and her husband were all State Supreme Court Justices?"

His eyebrows popped upward and then he scowled. "Are you threatening me? Because I have to tell you, I really don't like being threatened."

I shrugged. "Just telling you what you're up against before you make a mistake."

He laughed. "I'll give you this, kid, you got a lot of guts just walking in here this way."

I checked the reflection in the window without looking back, then drifted slowly to my right, so he'd have to get past the chair and that would slow him down. He was big but he also looked slow. Even so, I began to think maybe this hadn't been such a good idea.

"Hey, I'm not looking for trouble." I gestured with my head toward the goon. "Nobody comes looking for trouble with a guy who hires his muscle."

"Let me put it this way," Mr. Eddy said, "you are in way, way over your head here."

"That sounds pretty much like a threat."

"Take it any way you want."

I saw the guy start toward me and I knew what was coming. He wasn't gonna fight, he was just gonna grab my arm and hustle me out of the office, probably by the back door.

When he grabbed my arm, I grabbed his arm, stepped back and through and spun him around and drove his arm up between his shoulder blades, put one foot on his butt and shoved him up onto the desk and over into Eddy's lap. That tipped his chair over and they both banged back onto the floor and the goon's head made a sound like a turnip dropped from a church steeple when it hit the wall.

Eddy was trapped under the goon, who wasn't moving. But I could see he was breathing.

"I take threats very seriously," I said, and I walked around the desk, flipped open the goon's coat and pulled out the Glock he carried in a holster on his belt. Then I pulled out his wallet and dropped it on the desk and unloaded the gun.

I opened the wallet and pulled out what was inside. What

I was looking for wasn't there. He had no permit. So I picked up the phone and called Lieutenant Clark at the State Police office just down the road and told him what was going on.

Meanwhile, Eddy was swearing like a sailor after six months at sea, as he tried to get out from under the goon. It was pretty cool. I waited for the cops and it didn't take long.

Lt. Clark is a good guy and I'd gotten to know him a little because his son George is our left outside linebacker.

The short of it was he called for an ambulance for the goon who was still out cold, placed him under arrest for assault of a minor, and carrying a pistol without a permit.

And after he'd gotten everything sorted out, he took me outside and sat me in the cruiser.

"Okay, Charlie," he said. "You just bought yourself a lot of trouble, do you understand that?"

I nodded.

"But why? Why would you do that?"

"They're trying to drive Mrs. Parks into selling her land. They threatened her at least once."

"And you're helping Mrs. Parks."

"I am."

"Is this more of your famous detective work?"

I nodded.

"How many times do we have to tell you, Charlie, that you can't be doing stuff like this?"

"I hear it a lot," I said.

"But you don't quit."

"I came here to find out who those guys are and I found out. Now you know that probably the mob is fronting Greenfields the money to make this thing happen."

"I won't deny that," Lt. Clark said. "It smells like a money laundering operation."

"You think they'll send more of those guys down here?"

"You can count on it."

"Maybe you should alert the Steamship Authority to watch for 'em. I mean they aren't hard to spot. Just look for the shiny suits and the funny shoes."

He grinned and shook his head. "No wonder Bart said he was considering hiring you as a consultant."

"Did the DNA results come back yet."

He looked around at me. "As a matter of fact they just came in on my computer."

"And he's the Toledo guy?"

"Not a question. I'm just glad you didn't kill him."

"I didn't do anything," I said.

"And you didn't just throw a guy eighty pounds heavier than you over a desk, either. And there was the matter of the thugs from this past summer, too."

"If people would listen to me now and then, maybe it wouldn't come to something like that."

"You've made your point, Charlie. Now you have to back out of this and do it fast. Greenfields is now on my watch list and it'll shortly be on everyone's watch list. They made a big mistake today."

I didn't say what I knew. They'd made the mistake because I'm a kid in their eyes and they just didn't see it coming. It's a pretty good kind of camouflage. I was thinking I'd miss that when I grew up. But maybe by then I wouldn't need it. On the other hand, I *was* planning to be a lawyer.

"Maybe," I said, "they'll have to think things over. They probably thought everybody living here was a lightweight. People have made that mistake before."

He shook his head. "First they're gonna have to assess the damage. They'll pull Eddy and send in someone else. And here's what I'm telling you. Stay away! It's an order, Charlie. This is police business now."

"I got what I wanted," I said.

But I knew it wouldn't work that way. My guess was that these guys would go underground and it takes a lot of police work to keep track of something like that, and unless the state was willing to send in the High Crime Task Force, nothing would happen.

I was also betting that the next front man they sent would not be a crook. He'd be a straight up and down businessman and he would not have a bunch of goons around. Instead he'd have an accountant and a secretary and business manager and he would have done a lot of deals like this in the past. The cops could run every kind of background check they could think of and he'd come up clean.

Yeah, it was gonna get a lot harder because I was also guessing there would be another group that the new guy didn't even know about. Those would be the bad guys. They'd be professionals. But they would also be city guys. And they would not, after all, know what was really out in those woods.

I decided it was time to set a trap. I'm really good at traps. But the thing about a trap is that you have to know what you're setting out to trap. I knew. It was why I'd had to convince Mrs. Parks to leave.

20

Fessin' Up

Pete had gone and I sat at the desk, thinking ... always a dangerous business. You never know what might turn up. Even worse are the times when nothing turns up. Like now. Blank. Absolutely blank.

The intercom buzzed and it was Mom calling me in to dinner. I shut off the lights and walked to the house, waiting for my mind to kick in, but instead of the issue at hand, namely setting a trap to catch a rat, a pretty large rat, or maybe a lot of rats of ordinary human size, all I could think about was the homework I had to get done and then football practice in the afternoon.

But for my adventures in the afternoon, dinner would have gone smoothly.

"So," Mom said, "you're still at it."

I concentrated on my supper, waiting to find out how much she knew before I launched into a defense of what I'd done.

"Haven't you got anything to say?" she asked.

"What are we talking about here?" I said.

"You know perfectly well, Charlie. We had a call from the state police."

"Greenfields," I said.

"Yes, Greenfields. Do you have any idea how serious this is?"

Dad was saying nothing, which wasn't significant because he often waited until he had all the information before he said anything. Mom preferred the frontal attack, kind of like the guy who said, 'Damn the torpedoes, full speed ahead!' I like Dad's way best — most of the time.

"What do you want to know?" I couldn't avoid the discussion, so it was best to get it on the table.

"Everything."

"You must know most of it."

"I want to hear what you have to say."

So I told them. And I gave them the fully detailed description.

It left Mom shaking her head, wondering silently what kind of a monster she had raised.

"Those people were my clients and they were very good clients," she said.

"No they weren't. Didn't you tell us that they'd gone behind your back?"

"I might have gotten around that."

"But perhaps they're not the best sort of people to be dealing with," Dad said.

She looked up at him, "How can you say that? I don't know that they were anything but honest, honorable people."

"Well, that's certainly changed," Dad said.

"They haven't been convicted of anything," she said.

"And they won't be," I said. "They'll go back to Boston and they'll disappear until somebody drags the harbor."

Sometimes it's hard to know why people can't understand that there is another set of rules out there. I shook my head. "Mom, the guy that grabbed me was wearing a gun. He didn't have a permit for the gun because he's got a record. He's been in prison. I don't think the average developer has a guy like that just hanging around the office."

"Where's Mrs. Parks?" Dad asked.

"Arizona, with her son, Walter."

"What made her decide to leave?" Mom asked. "She'd have been perfectly safe here."

I looked at Dad and he understood.

"I gather," he said, "that Charlie convinced her it might be best."

"Eddy had talked to her about selling the land and he brought his thug. She had forgotten the thug until we talked and then she remembered where she'd seen people like that before. In criminal court. Once she remembered that, she left."

"Who knows that?" Dad asked.

"The three of us. No one else."

"They'll send more people," Dad said.

I nodded. "That's what Lt. Clark said. But at least they'll be watched."

"I don't think we've seen the last of them," Dad said.

I rubbed the back of my neck. Not a good sign.

"Charlie," Mom said, "you have got to stop this!"

I said nothing.

"Did you hear me?"

"Yup."

"Well?"

"What can I say? Mrs. Parks is gone and the Greenfields guys are gone. Not much likely to happen now."

I could feel Dad's eyes trying to bore a hole into my brain. But by then they both knew I wasn't going to commit to anything, either one way or the other. I couldn't. I still had to solve the mystery of just what was in the woods. Maybe that was over too. Or maybe they'd move the whole operation so far underground that nobody could find it.

My brain had reengaged and bit by bit a plan fell into place. Tonight. I'd start tonight because they wouldn't have sent anyone down here that quickly and I could count on getting set up without having to worry about being watched.

Which explains why I went out for pizza at ten, something I did often enough so it raised no eyebrows.

And this time Pete went with me. No fog. Absolutely clear and cool.

"So what have you got in mind here?" Pete asked.

"Just a reconnoiter job."

"A what?"

"I want to see what's going on at the house, whether anyone's been there. I've got a key."

"How do you tell if anyone's been there?"

"Basic detective work. I'll show you when we get there. It'll make more sense."

I started with the fertilizer I'd spread and we hit pay dirt immediately. There were tracks up to both the front and back doors and some by the windows. But these were ordinary, human-sized footprints.

"These tracks are a couple of days old," I said. "See how the edges are sort of rounded? If the tracks were fresh, those edges would be sharp and the outlines of the heels would be sharply defined."

Next, I showed him where I had placed dampened threads at the bottom of the doors and windows. None of them had been disturbed.

"That's pretty cool stuff, Charlie, just like James Bond,

huh?" He pointed to the canvas bag I had slung over my shoulder. "Whatcha got in there?"

"Tools of the trade." I opened the garage door, drove my truck in and closed the door. From there we walked into the hall that led to the house. I turned on the lights. "What we're gonna do is plug in these timers all through the house so lights go on and off at given intervals." I opened the bag, looked at the labels on the timers, and gave him four. "These are for the living room. Plug them into the wall outlets and then plug the lamp cords into them. The one with the red panel on it is for the lamp by that chair." I pointed to the big overstuffed swivel chair that sat by the big atrium doors.

While he plugged those in, I set the stereo to PBS, and plugged it into the timer.

Then we did the bathroom and the bedroom and kitchen. Everything was set in phases. When the living room lights went out, the bedroom lights went on and then the lights in the bathroom, and then those lights went out and finally the bedroom lights. All of it was set on the timers. The kitchen timers were slightly different because they were equipped with light sensors, so on a dark day, during those times when someone was likely to be in the kitchen, the lights would turn on and then turn off at a given interval.

"So what we're trying to do here is make it look like someone is home, is that it?"

"Yeah."

"And by setting the lights the way you have, you create a pattern that might duplicate the way someone lives when they're here."

I nodded.

"Why?"

"Now it gets a little iffy," I said.

"Iffy?"

"Take a guess."

"With you? No way? " he scratched his head. "Okay, you want someone to think Mrs. Parks is still here, right?"

I nodded.

"That's as far as I can get."

"Think about it as third and long."

He grinned. "Fake the run, drop back, fake a pass long and then go short to the tight end on a delayed start from the line."

"Or maybe the quarterback draw, or maybe a timing pass."

"Anyone of them would work." He laughed. "But we're not talking football here."

"We're talking drawing out the other side, making them commit and catching them in the act."

"Using a fake so they don't see it coming."

"Yeah, exactly."

I could see Pete was about through with my metaphorical romp, so I explained.

"My guess is that, given the chance, and given the circumstances, somebody might want to get rid of Mrs. Parks. And the guys we're dealing with here wouldn't think twice about whacking someone, even an old lady. But they need to make it look right. For example, it would be easy enough for a sniper to set up somewhere in the woods and pick her off but that would look like a planned hit and it would tip off the good guys ... us.

"So instead, they need to make it look like a common, run-of-the-mill kind of crime. It'll still raise suspicion, but the cops will only see it one way because it will be designed to fit their expectations of what happens when someone confronts an armed burglar."

Pete grinned. "Okay, now I get it. They watch the lights, figure out when she's in her bedroom, break in and when she confronts them, they shoot her. Then they steal some stuff, mess the place up, and to the cops it looks like a robbery-murder."

"Right."

"Can I point out something?" Pete said.

"Sure."

"She isn't here."

"But she will be, sort of. I'll make it look like she's in bed, asleep with the lights on."

"If they shoot her in bed, it won't work, will it?"

"Follow me."

We walked into the bedroom, and I reset the timer so the lights came on. Then I clapped my hands together hard and the lights went out. "That's what'll happen when the gun goes off. The shooter will suddenly be in the dark and he'll get out of there fast, thinking that maybe he triggered some kind of alarm he didn't know about."

"So he runs off. How does he get caught?"

"I'll be watching. When the gun goes off I call the cops and tell them where to intercept the guy.

"In the radio next to the bed there's a camera. It's connected to a recording unit. The switch is in a laser beam across the door to the room."

"That oughta get it done."

"If I've thought of everything."

"When do you think they'll turn up?" Pete asked.

"Soon. They need to get this done and since the little incident at the Greenfields office, they can't waste any time."

"What little incident? I haven't heard about this."

So, I told him.

"Another hood? You got to take down another hood. Why didn't you bring me along? Man, I love beating on those guys!"

"I didn't know, Pete. I just went there to poke around a little and the next thing I knew the guy grabbed my arm and I stopped him."

"Kind of like calling an audible."

"Only I was on the defensive side, so it was more like reading the play."

"Do I get to talk about this?" Pete said.

"Nope. Nobody's talking."

"Com'on, Charlie, get real. By tomorrow the whole Island will know."

He was right. There had been at least three cruisers and the ambulance and when that many emergency people turn up, things get out. And, after all, my truck had been parked right out front and everybody knows that truck.

The last thing I did was back Mrs. Parks's Mercedes into the drive and close the door. She almost never used the garage.

And then we headed home. Setting a trap is a lot like fishing with bait. You put it out there and wait. Most of the time I'm not patient enough to fish with bait. Not enough activity. But sometimes ... sometimes it's no bad thing to just sit in the boat, rocking in the waves, put your hands behind your head, and wait.

21

Right Place, Right Time

I was under suspicion at home and that was making it harder to come up with logical reasons to go out at night. I resorted to pizza. Pete and I had been going for a pizza at night maybe three times a week so that was first on my list.

I needed some pizza. It had not been one of my better days at practice. Usually, I never dropped a pass, but that afternoon I'd dropped three of them. It was like I had oil on my gloves.

Coach never said a thing. To make things worse, I missed my blocks on four or five running plays and I'd never missed a single time before. Clearly, I was distracted.

But the pizza helped and Pete and I had no trouble wolfing down a couple of extra large models with everything but anchovies. I never eat rotten fish.

Pete finished his last piece and leaned back in his chair. "So, anybody whacked Mrs. Parks yet?"

"I'm going out there to check after we finish."

"You want me to go?"

"I didn't think you wanted to."

"I changed my mind."

I put the truck in the garage and then we went outside to check for tracks and I was about to switch on my light when I heard an outboard out on the pond.

We walked into the woods down to where we could see the water and in the moonlight we watched a skiff coming across, aimed right at Mrs. Parks's dock.

It carried two men, one running the large outboard and another sitting facing forward.

"Company coming," I said and pointed off to the left. "Let's circle that way so we can see what happens.

"We stay out of sight, though, right?"

"We don't move until the boat leaves with both men."

Quickly, we worked our way down through the woods, taking no great care to be quiet because there was no way the guys in the boat could hear us over the sound of the motor.

We took up a position back in the woods, screened by the brush and the trees and waited. The only lights still on were in the bedroom.

The engine shut off and one of the men came up from

the landing, but well off to the right. He waited there, watching the house and after about ten minutes he moved in, walking across the back lawn, slipped a card into the latch on the atrium doors, and stepped inside.

Perhaps a minute later he came back out, running now, not even closing the door behind him. Which meant he knew he'd been set up. "Start the motor," he shouted and we heard the outboard start and then he ran out onto the dock and jumped into the boat. The last thing we heard him say was ... "We been set up! Get us out of here!"

We ran back through the woods and around to the front of the house and the garage.

I could smell the gunpowder from the time we opened the door into the back hall from the garage. In the bedroom, the lights had come back on and we could see where he'd thrown back the covers on the bed to reveal the pillows we'd put there to make it look like someone was in the bed. There were five bullet holes through the pillows.

"How come we didn't hear anything?" Pete asked.

"Silencer." I pointed to the holes. "Probably a .22 auto which by now is somewhere at the bottom of Great Pond."

I punched in Bart's number on my cell and told him what had happened and where I was headed.

We climbed into the truck, backed out of the garage and I pushed the button to close the door and tore off down the dirt road.

"They came straight across the pond so there's only one place they could have launched. We'll wait out of sight and get the license number on the truck. It's probably stolen, but if we can get a description of the truck and the tag number the cops can nail them before they get to the ferry."

"You do think of everything, don't you?" Pete said.

"Sometimes. But all we've proven is that someone tried to kill Mrs. Parks. We need to get these guys so we can connect them to whoever put out the contract."

"How can we do that?"

I chuckled. "We can't. I'd have to go to Boston and take on the mob. Anything off-Island is somebody else's problem." I glanced at him. "Besides, I'm not crazy."

"Sure fooled a lot of people," Pete said.

"They really thought I was a nutbag, huh?"

"That was pretty much the general opinion."

"Is it changing?"

"Yeah, but slowly. Saving the Kings put marks in both columns. But football helped big time. It can be understood. But a ninja killer coming from the dark ... a thing like that makes people nervous."

"It even makes me nervous," I said.

"Why do I not believe that?"

"You should."

"I've seen you in action, Charlie, remember?"

"Once things start, I'm okay. Before that my hands sweat

and sometimes my legs shake."

"You mean you're just a normal guy, after all?"

"Sure. Perfectly normal."

"Except around girls."

"Perfectly normal. I don't know what's going on."

"Hey, you're not alone. Remember, like I told you, just don't talk."

"It's kinda like the way you behave after a cop reads you your Miranda rights."

"What?"

"Anything you say can be used as evidence against you."

Pete laughed. "Exactly right."

I parked the truck at one of the cottages that was closed up during the week in September, and then we walked back out to the road and hid at a spot where the road took a sharp curve to the left, forcing them to slow.

Minutes later we heard the truck coming fast. It worked perfectly. It was either slow down or go off the road into the trees and we got a license number from the truck and a perfect description. All in all a good day.

I dropped Pete at his house and drove over to the police station.

Bart took me into his office and we sat in the two easy chairs at the end by the window.

"Well, we got 'em," he said, "but we're a little unclear on the charges."

I gave him the key to the house. "There's a camera," I said and then I told him where to find it and how it worked and how we'd set up the timing on the house lights.

The next day Bart told me that not only was the video perfect but the shooter was a guy named The Rat and the Boston P.D., the State Police, and the F.B.I. had been after him for a long time. Made me feel pretty good.

I didn't say anything to my folks. I figured Bart would talk to Dad and it was better if he heard it that way.

22

Another Side Of Charlie (by Pete)

I had to tell you about this because Charlie wouldn't, at least not the way I can. And anyway, it's about Charlie and sometimes he's pretty modest about what he can do.

It's also about the game on Saturday. It was away at Westwood High, and they had hammered us the year before. But that was when most of our offensive line had been sophomores and now all but one of those guys were juniors and they were a lot bigger and tougher, and a lot nastier.

We wanted revenge.

We got the kickoff and ended up on our own forty-eight yard line, in terrific field position. I called Charlie's number and he made a perfect cut to the middle for a quick look-in and I hit him right in the hands and … he dropped it.

He'd been doing that all week in practice, but somehow

I didn't think he'd drop one in a game. When he came back to the huddle I told him to forget about it, as did all the other guys. Heck we still had two downs to push it ten yards.

Except that we couldn't. They had a guy covering C.D., who was almost as fast and he never bought a single fake. In the line they had a nose guard the size of a small bulldozer and a middle linebacker almost as big and both of them were very quick.

They stuffed us.

Worse, they ran back our punt for a touchdown and things began to look pretty grim. By the end of the first quarter, we were down 21-0 and we hadn't made a single first down. It just sucked the energy right out of everyone.

I saw Charlie talking to Coach as we changed from offense to defense and then he ran out onto the field with the defense and settled into the right outside linebacker's spot. Usually, Rich Younts played there, but he'd strained his knee on the second series of plays and the kid Coach had put in was a sophomore and really green, and worse, scared.

Westwood also had a passing game. Their quarterback had a good strong arm and their receivers ran fast, tight routes. That's where they were killing us.

On the first snap, the quarterback dropped back to throw and I saw Charlie hit the defensive guy in front of him and knock the guy absolutely flat, and then he jumped over him and slammed into the quarterback and the ball went flying and Charlie kept right on going, scooping up the ball, and heading for the endzone. Just like that we got seven points back, but more importantly, you could feel the energy surge up and down our side of the field.

We kicked off and Charlie, who had never been on a kick-off team, came down the field like a rocket, blew through two blocks, hit the ball carrier, and punched the ball out of his arms and Jon fell on the fumble.

We started at their thirty-yard line and in the huddle I called Charlie's number. He was in the zone, absolutely, totally in the zone. When a guy is there, you call his number until he can't run.

It was a sideline pattern and Charlie simply turned the defense the wrong way, picked off the ball with one hand and spun out of the next tackle and stiff-armed the free safety, pinwheeling the guy, and trotted into the endzone.

He made it all look so easy. And the thing is, it wasn't easy. He'd just made three unbelievable plays and it took the wind out of Westwood.

It's called momentum, the big "mo" and now we had it and they didn't.

What's more, their coach had to do something to contain Charlie and he went to double coverage and when I went up to the line and stood behind the center I saw it coming and I called an audible, making C.D. the primary receiver. I love calling audibles. It's like real football.

C.D. went down the field so fast you could almost see cartoon speed lines in the air behind him and I just threw it up and let him run under it. I never saw a guy in football camp that could have caught up to the ball I threw, but C.D. is so fast he almost overran the pass.

By the half, we were up seven and went tearing off the field, even as the guys from Westwood dragged themselves off to the locker room.

We weren't as hot in the second half, and I'll say this, the Westwood coach pumped a lot of life back into his team at halftime. But it wasn't nearly enough. They scored all right, but it was an uphill struggle because Charlie was still playing outside linebacker and after their quarterback had been sacked three times, he kept flicking his eyes toward Charlie and it caused him to lose focus and his passes went everywhere but to his receivers.

When you play quarterback you can't think about being hit. You can only think about your receivers and who's covered and who's open. He had a bad day.

The third quarter ended with the score tied, mostly because their monster guy in the middle of the defense began to blow through, and twice he sacked me. Not only was this guy big, but he was quick. And suddenly instead of stepping up into the pocket I was scrambling.

Through most of the fourth quarter nobody did much. Time after time both teams went three downs and punted.

159

With about four minutes to go, we had Charlie go back to receive the punt. It was a lot to ask, because he'd been playing both offense and defense for most of the game, and most guys would be dragging. That's why you get yourself into the best shape you can. Some games are a matter of who's still standing at the end.

It was a nasty punt, short and squibbing across the ground and the most you hope for with a punt like that is that it doesn't hit you accidentally and give the other team a chance to recover the ball.

So what does Charlie do? I still don't believe he did it. He scooped up the ball with one hand, spun away from the tackler, stiff-armed the next guy and picked up nearly thirty yards on the runback.

It left us on our own forty with plenty of time to score.

But Westwood was not cooperating. They could smell blood just as we could and they came at us with everything they had. They knocked down one pass, they stuffed a run and that left us with third and long.

It is where quarterbacks don't want to wind up on any series of downs. The completion rate, even for the pros, is not good. Third and twelve is what we were facing.

The coach sent in a play, a look-in to the tight end, Jon. A good call. Westwood would probably blitz here and that meant sending their linebackers and that would leave Jon open in the middle. I liked it.

And I liked being under the gun. Third and long is what separates the sheep from the goats, the men from the boys, the wheat from the chaff (whatever that is). It's where the guy with the cool head, the guy who doesn't rattle, has a chance to take away the game.

I know I'm blowing my own horn here, but hey, situations like that are what I like best about football. Either you cut it or you don't and "don't" never entered my mind until I pulled up into the shotgun and looked over the defense. No blitz. They knew it was a pass and their coach had every defender back and nobody even leaning toward the line.

I changed the play. I called a quarterback draw. I needed twelve yards for a first down and to get that I had to have somebody block the middle linebacker.

Normally Jon would have gotten the call, but I wanted him to go downfield in case everything collapsed so I'd still have him to throw to.

Cool. You have to be cool to pull that play off. I took the snap, faked a throw to Jon over the middle and that froze the middle linebacker and the guys in our line, steered their blocks and I spun around and into the open and that's when Charlie hit the middle linebacker from the side and sent him flying out of the play, even as he rolled onto his feet and took aim on the free safety who was coming up fast.

The guy never had a chance. Charlie took his feet out from under him and I ran. Man, did I run. But hey, I'm not fast. Everybody knows that, and I was a long way from the endzone.

They caught me at the ten, two of them, and I dragged them for another three yards before I went down.

I shouted for the huddle, wanting to get another play off fast before their coach could call a time out, and it worked.

It was a timing play. I took the snap and floated a soft pass to the far corner of the endzone and right into C.D.'s hands. Talk about sweet!

The bus ride home was bedlam. I never had a better bus ride. In our league we were now the team to beat and there were only two other teams, Somerset and Blue Hills, that we had to worry about.

Now, here's the even more surprising part of this. In the locker room, Charlie was the life of the party, joking and laughing and ragging on guys like he'd been doing this all his life. I never saw anything like it.

I mean we're talking Charles Oliver Jones, private investigator, here, probably the biggest outcast in the whole school and all of a sudden, he's one of the guys and not lording it over anyone, or making a big deal about the way he'd played. He was getting everyone into it, getting them ready to play at another level.

He was our leader. And to tell you the truth, I was kind of jealous. And I would have been really jealous, except that it was Charlie, and because of the way he went about it. When we left the locker room, he'd made it clear that I had won the game.

And he kept saying over and over, "third and long ... third and long ..." He passed out credit to everyone. He seemed to remember every play and he let everyone know that we were a team.

We were sitting in his truck, riding home and I turned in the seat and said: "What made you go in on defense?"

He shrugged. "I was pissed, that's all. I was dropping passes and I wasn't in the game. My head was off somewhere else so I thought maybe if I started hitting people it would help me focus."

"Where did you get an idea like that?"

"Karate tournaments. I performed best after I'd taken a hit. It woke something up inside."

"Remind me not to piss you off, okay?"

He laughed. "But you never get ruffled. You're always under control. Like that audible you called. You read the defense, changed the play, and it changed the game. And talk about a gutsy call. Third and long, a defining moment, and you call a play that maybe is good for five yards."

"They were leaning the wrong way. But the thing is, everybody did their job. You made two crushing blocks, the line pulled back just right, Jon froze the linebackers. It was awesome!"

"I don't know how you do that," he said. "I couldn't do

that. I can run, I can fake, and I can hit pretty hard." He shook his head. "No way could I just stand there and find the receiver and let fly, knowing that I was gonna get hit."

"It's part of playing quarterback," I said. "That's why you need to have size and strength."

Suddenly he slapped the top of the steering wheel with his left hand. "Man, do I like playing football!"

Probably I should have seen that change coming, but Charlie is very hard to read. He's been working on that for years. He can be absolutely stone-faced. On the other hand, I'd known him my whole life and I should have seen it.

And my not having seen it raised an interesting and uncomfortable question. Did I not see things in other people because I was too focused on myself?

Once you ask something like that, it changes your perspective. You just see things differently. Think about this. All those years I had known Charlie, I thought he was one thing and in seconds it all changed and he was way different.

Was that what adults meant by growing up? It seemed like it might be and if it was, I decided that growing up offered a lot more than I thought it had. Suddenly I realized that I was asking questions I had never posed before.

I just hoped it would help me on the SATs.

There is one more thing to talk about and that was the hit man. Once again Charlie's detective work had paid off. The guy was in the top ten of the FBI's most-wanted list!

And a kid on Martha's Vineyard nails him. Is that out there, or what? Of course it wasn't any regular sort of everyday kid, it was Charles Oliver Jones.

The weird thing is that nobody seemed to know anything about it. Charlie tipped off the cops, they made the arrests and turned the guys over to the state cops, who had them off-Island before the newspapers knew a thing.

The story turned up a day later in the Boston Globe and all it said was that the guys were being held for about a million in bail. It said nothing about the Vineyard.

And that's the way Charlie liked it. He didn't care about the publicity, in fact, he didn't want any publicity. He said it would "compromise" his freedom to act.

Well, football players know what the word compromise means, but I had never heard it used that way so I had to go look it up. Hanging with Charlie was not exactly a bed of roses, but there's this to say. Nobody before had ever shown so much interest in my education.

The result was that I had begun to worry about my education. I mean, hey, I was going to college and as long as I was going, it made sense to learn something. Not that I went around shouting this from the rooftops, because a thing like that can compromise your reputation.

Naw, you never admit to a thing like that. It's like talking to girls ... you say nothing.

23

Digging Deeper

Monday, at dinner I found out that Greenfields had decided to sell their property and they'd listed it with Mom. I gave her Walter Parks number and she called that night. The next day she sent a purchase contract to Mrs. Parks.

And that was the end of that, except for a couple of nagging little details such as what had happened to the monster in the big boots and my wanting to get a look at the sasquatch. I didn't doubt for a second he was there.

The next morning it rained and the fog closed in and we were socked in solid. That night the fog hung on, getting thicker by the hour and I had no choice. I had to see whether the monster had shown up. I was pretty sure the one with the boots was gone, because I was pretty sure he'd been part of the Greenfields scam to drive Mrs. Parks into selling out.

At nine o'clock, I parked my car well up the road and walked in. All the lights in the house were out and I chose a spot where I could watch the back of the house, close enough so I could see through the fog, which meant I was pretty close because the fog was thick.

This time I'd brought a folding camp stool. You can wait a lot longer if you're comfortable. That also leads to thinking and I have to say that my life was getting weirder by the second. Most private eyes make a living by working for lawyers who handle divorce cases. I didn't want any part of that. It's a small island and from what I knew about divorce stuff, it's very messy and very personal.

I'd had three calls in the past two days from women and men wanting me to gather evidence they could use in divorce court. I'd turned them all down. Maybe I'm like the famous Spenser in the novels by Robert B. Parker. He doesn't do divorce work either.

But in my case it's a little different. Two of the three people who called had kids I knew. No way could I be responsible for wrecking their lives.

So, there I was, sitting and thinking about all manner of things and that went on for an hour and a half and nothing moved, nothing stirred.

I made one check around the house before I left and there were no new footprints. To tell the truth, I was kind of disappointed. In fact, it was kind of depressing in an odd sort of way. It was like losing a friend.

Wednesday morning broke clear and dry and phones were ringing all over the Island. The Toledo serial killer had escaped from the hospital.

I think they must've sent in every cop in the Commonwealth of Massachusetts. There were cops crawling over the island like an invasion of army ants.

I got called to the office to talk with Chief Espinoza and a state police captain in private. What I got was a warning. I was to stay out of their way. I was not to do anything, and especially I wasn't to go out at night in my ninja suit. They were afraid I'd get whacked by one of their own guys.

To tell the truth, it had never occurred to me. It was a police job and once the police are in, I'm out and I stay out … well, as long as they get something done. And with that many guys they couldn't miss.

That night, sitting in the office, working on my AP history homework, my mind kept drifting. Usually, I can sit and focus and absorb what I need, and I can do that for an hour or more before I need to get up and stretch. But now I was up and down, back and forth, and I knew why. Something was twisting and turning in my head, trying to work it's way to the surface. And there was also the matter of Friday's game.

No small thing.

I called Pete.

It couldn't have taken him two minutes to get there.

"'Sup, Dude?"

"I needed to talk."

He grabbed a soda from the fridge. "You want one?"

"I'm okay."

He dropped onto the couch. "So ... talk."

"I'm trying to remember something, something important and I can't get it to come to the surface."

"What's it about?"

"I'm not sure."

"The fog thingy?"

"No, not that, though that's still an issue."

"The Toledo killer?"

That stopped me and I felt something connect and disappear. "It could be that."

"The whole Island's talking about it."

"Sure. What else?"

"Hot stuff ... killer escapes from the hospital and nobody can find him. Lot of people won't sleep much tonight."

I grinned. "You got that right.

"Maybe you're focusing too hard."

I nodded. "The thing is, I have the feeling that I need to know this and I need to know it now!" I walked over to the desk and dropped into the chair and let it tip back so I could swing my feet up onto the desk. "At a time like this in novels, the private eye pulls out a bottle of whiskey."

"But you don't drink."

"Plenty of time for that when I get to college."

"Not during football." He grinned. "Later it'll be ... party time, man."

"Why not?"

He looked up at me, lifting his head from the pillow on the couch, his eyebrows arched. "Charlie Jones, P.A.?"

I didn't get it. "P.A.? What's a P.A.?"

"Party animal, Dude."

I shook my head and grinned as visions of the movie *Animal House* drifted through my mind. Would it really be like that? Somehow, I couldn't see myself living that way. And then, out of nowhere, it connected.

The night I followed the Toledo killer, I'd been impressed by the way he used the available cover to trail his victims without being seen. I could remember thinking that he'd done this sort of thing a lot, but I had also noticed that the cover he used was almost always either trees or shrubs. That led to the notion that maybe he was comfortable in the woods.

On the other hand he would still need to get off the island and that meant taking the ferry. Oak Bluffs was out. It was wide open. What about Vineyard Haven? Still pretty open and certainly nothing nearby that qualified as woodlands.

Of course he could always steal a boat but I wondered how much a guy from Toledo would know about boats. No answer. I didn't know whether he came from there or had migrated there. But stealing a boat would be risky because the Coast Guard would be out in force and they would stop and check every boat.

No. The best way was to take the ferry. And that meant he would have to stow away. I ruled out cars because the only way he could be sure that any particular car was headed off-island was to find one at the Steamship Authority parking lot in the loading line, and not only was that lot well lighted, but the cops would be everywhere.

"Yo, Earth to Charlie ..."

I looked up quickly.

"What are you thinking about?" Pete asked.

"The Toledo guy. I think he likes the woods. I think he's used to the woods. But the thing is, he has to get off the island. My guess is he'd try to stow away, but I'm not sure how he could manage that."

"If it was me, I'd use a truck."

"Good call," I said. "One of those tractor-trailer rigs, even a big box truck would do as long as he could get into it without being seen."

"I've never noticed what kind of trucks come and go."

"You mean like trailers or box or big vans, or ..."

"No, I meant what they carry."

"Most of the big trucks bring a load of something over and go back empty. Maybe they all do."

"Wouldn't it be kind of hard to hide in an empty truck?"

I crossed to the fridge. "You want a soda?"

"Yeah."

I took out a couple of Cokes and handed one to Pete. "So it would have to be some kind of truck that brought something back. Suppose it was a truck making a delivery here and then making a delivery somewhere else?"

"Why not?"

"You wanna go for a ride?"

"Sure."

We checked the ferry schedule, carried our drinks out to my truck, got in, and headed over to Vineyard Haven where most all of the trucks came and went.

"How're your hands?" Pete asked.

"Fine."

"Won't be dropping any passes?"

I laughed. "My hands are fine. But I twisted my knee when I fell down the stairs this after ..."

"What!" He went off like a rocket.

"Whoa, Whoa there, big fella. It's a joke."

"Damn, Charlie, don't do that to me, okay? The whole season flashed before my eyes."

We parked in the lot by the grocery store and walked down to the Steamship Authority and sat on one of the benches like we had come to meet someone. There were twelve semi's waiting to load.

"What, exactly, are we looking for," Pete asked.

"Some of these guys come over on Monday and drop a trailer and then go somewhere else to pick up an empty trailer. Mostly they're carrying building supplies."

"How do you know that?"

"I put up and take down signs for my Mom's business and … " Suddenly it came clear. "And I've watched guys unload doors and windows and insulation and shingles and here's something I just thought of. A lot of that stuff comes in on pallets and they take the pallets back with them. I can remember watching the trucker lash them to the sides of the truck to keep them from flying around inside. They stack them near the back of the truck."

"Do they take anything else back?"

"Sure, all kinds of boxes and packaging materials because it's easier to get rid of that stuff on the mainland."

"Wouldn't that be a good place to hide?"

"Even better, how about this? A lot of those semi's sit in places surrounded by woods. They lock them up at night, but I'll bet once they're empty, they don't bother to lock the doors." I stood up. "Let's take a walk."

24

Thinking Pays Off

"Maybe we oughta call the cops," Pete said.

"We'll just take a look. The guy was in the hospital and he can't be in very good shape."

"Maybe he's got a gun."

"Where would he get a gun?"

He grabbed my arm and stopped me. "Let's think this over a minute. We got a game to play on Friday and that gives us only a day or so to recover from a gunshot wound. Not long enough, right?"

I grinned. "Right."

"So we do the smart thing and turn it over to the cops, right?"

"Nope."

"Com'on, Charlie, wake up and smell the coffee here."

"Have you got your cell phone with you?"

"Yeah."

"If we find a truck I want to look into, you back off and stay where you can see what's going on. If I need you to call the police, I'll holler, okay?"

"Why do you want to do this?"

"It's not that. I just don't want to call in the cops unless there's a reason. I hate the thought of crying wolf."

"And if he's got a gun?"

"I'll be ready."

"Oh, man, You can't do stuff like this during the season!"

"Nothing's gonna happen, Pete."

"You're not even scared, are you?"

I shrugged. "Just enough to be ready. Look, this guy had all kinds of tubes stuck in him at the hospital and right now he's got to be hurting. He may not even be conscious."

"But probably his trigger finger's still working."

"Give me your cell phone." I took it and punched all but the last digit of the chief's number. "The last digit is six. If I holler, you punch in a six and Espinoza will answer in a rush. You tell him you're with me and we've got the Toledo guy."

"Which truck are you going to try?"

I pointed to a truck up ahead in the first boarding lane. "That one. See what it says on the side? Herrett's Building Supplies. It's the only one."

"Where do you want me?"

I pointed down the line to a red Chevvy pickup. "Behind that truck. I'll wait 'til you're in place."

"Okay."

Once he was safely behind the pickup, I walked to the back of the trailer, reached up, and slowly opened the latch, hoping it wouldn't squeal. But it had been well greased and I loosed the latch, opened the door just enough to get in, and popped up into the truck. I pulled it closed and pulled out my powerful tac light, and a throwing star.

I stayed absolutely still, listening, focused on the last stack of pallets. If he was here that's where he'd be. I moved into the truck a few feet a time, stopping to listen. When I reached the last stack. I heard someone breathing very slowly. I stood up, stepped around the pallets, and flicked on the light.

He lay on his back, flat on the floor, his hands spread to the sides. He was either sleeping or passed out and I put the throwing star back into my jacket and unhooked the cuffs from my belt. I kept to his right side, grabbed his left hand, dragged it behind his back, and handcuffed it to his right.

Still, he didn't move. I checked his pulse and it felt very weak. I pulled out my cell phone and called the chief, then I went through his pockets and sure enough he was armed, an old Smith & Wesson thirty-eight. I assumed he must have stolen it from the same place he had stolen the clothes.

I emptied the gun, dropped the cartridges into my pocket, set the gun on top of the pallet stack by the door, then dropped out onto the parking lot, swung the open door to the side of the trailer and hooked it so it would stay open. Finally, I walked to where Pete was waiting.

"What happened?" he asked.

"He's out cold," I said. "Good thing too." I showed him the cartridges. "You were right about the gun."

"I told you, didn't I? I told you he had a gun!"

"Yeah, Dude, you did. Absolutely."

By then the sirens were howling like a wolf pack.

The state police got there first and you'd have thought I was the bad guy.

"Where is he?" a tall trooper asked.

I pointed to the truck, the door still open.

"Is he armed?"

"The gun is on the top of the last stack of pallets. I emptied it. After I cuffed him."

"Who are you?"

"Charles Oliver Jones …" I was tempted to add private investigator, but these guys were way too pumped. They had to be. They were searching for a killer.

And then the chief showed up and I told him what to expect. "I think you'll need an ambulance. His pulse is pretty weak."

He grinned. "Nice piece of work, Charlie. Maybe later you can tell me how you figured it out."

"Pete helped me," I said.

"No, I didn't," Pete said. "All I said was the guy probably had a gun."

The chief shook his head. "Which, of course, he ignored."

"It was okay. I figured he couldn't be in very good shape."

Chief Espinoza looked right at me. "Pretty big risk," he said.

"I told him," Pete said. "I told him that the guy's trigger finger was probably still working."

I pulled a throwing star from my pocket and showed it to them. "He'd been sitting in the dark. And I had a very bright light, bright enough to blind him. I held the light off to my left and if he'd moved I'd have hit him with the star."

"And you're good enough to do that?" the chief said.

Pete jumped in. "Absolutely, Chief. It's awesome!"

"Show me sometime, okay?"

"Sure."

Cape Cod Tech won the toss and elected to receive and for a second, when they formed a wedge in front of their runner, I thought they might just take it into the endzone.

They didn't, but they had made it to our thirty-five. It left them with a lot of options.

I was still playing linebacker on defense but I wasn't terribly optimistic. These guys were big. We set up three down linemen and three linebackers, giving us one more guy in the secondary to defend against the pass. It's sometimes called a nickel defense because you have five guys back.

Coach was expecting them to pass. So was everybody else. But I had an idea they might try something unusual, especially on first down, so I didn't rush the passer. Instead I fought off a block and stayed home.

The quarterback rolled to his right as if he were getting ready to pass and then a wide receiver tore in behind him and took the handoff. The Statue of Liberty play. Their fullback came right at me, but I had already moved, not at the ball carrier but toward a point to his left near the sideline.

What that did was allow me to work at a slant against their blockers and it kept them from getting any kind of a direct hit. I spun past the fullback and then cut in my afterburners. Man did I nail that guy. I hit him a yard behind the line of scrimmage and knocked the ball loose and scrambled after it, but it went out of bounds.

Stuffing the offense is a very good way to start a game. They were looking at second down with eleven yards to go instead of ten.

Now, they had to try a pass. So, on the snap, I spun around my blocker, spun around the fullback and leaped just as the quarterback threw the ball. I got my fingertips on it, just enough to force the ball sideways and onto the ground.

In the defensive huddle I told the guys that they'd probably try rolling to the right away from my side of the line. I told them to line up the way we usually did but on the snap everyone was to go to their left and try to find an opening.

Our defensive line is very good. They are tough and fast and two of our down linemen blasted past the defense and the quarterback never had a chance. All he could do was tuck the ball in tight to keep anyone from knocking it loose, and take the sack.

Tech was now back at midfield with no chance of kicking a field goal and they had to punt. Talk about sweet. In three plays we had driven them out of our territory.

Our offense came onto the field about as high as you can get. And of course the word on Pete was out and they were looking pass all the way and as a result we ran two running plays and picked up twenty-three yards and two first downs.

And then we went without a huddle, something we'd been working on a lot in practice.

I took an inside route and C. D. ran a post pattern and Pete just laid it out there for him and C. D. picked it out of the air and ran on into the end zone without anyone laying a hand on him.

After that things got a lot tougher. Tech began to recover their confidence and they managed several first downs, but they never got past our forty.

We were running a lot of stunts and fakes on defense and their quarterback only ran the plays the coach called. He had a good enough arm, but either he couldn't read the defense fast enough to call a new play at the line of scrimmage or his coach didn't allow him that kind of latitude.

But we couldn't score either. Their pass defense, after that one mistake, was the best we'd seen and I was double covered all the time and C.D. just couldn't get open.

We were still ahead seven to nothing in the fourth quarter when our punter misfired and Tech ended up with the ball on our thirty-two.

Five plays later they scored.

With two minutes to go we ran back the kickoff to our own forty. They knew we'd pass. We had to because there was so little time left. And by then they knew our patterns, so I pulled Pete and C.D. aside.

What we did was switch the pass routes so that C.D. took the inside, a slant up the middle, and I faked to the inside and ran a fly down the sideline to draw the deep coverage. Their safety was fast enough to cover C.D., but the other guys weren't.

Pete faked a run, raced to his right, and fired a rocket to C.D. just as he broke past the coverage, and I laid a good clean block on the safety

And on one more Saturday we walked away winners. Such a thing had not been seen in a long time on the Vineyard.

25

A Grisley Discovery

Sunday morning I got up very early, determined to walk Mrs. Park's land from top to bottom and side to side. And this time I went armed. I had my shotgun, which I can, after all, carry because I have a hunting license. One small detail, the fact that the hunting season wasn't open yet, I allowed myself to overlook.

Which was why I had to start early while my folks were still asleep. I didn't want to go through any long explanations about the shotgun.

It's a semiautomatic Browning Auto-5 and I loaded it with double ought buckshot. That would be even harder to explain. Those are the loads you use for deer and we were a long way from deer season.

On the other hand, the wardens were pretty busy with

the Fishing Derby, which I too planned to get busy with once I'd satisfied myself that the guy with the big boots was gone.

I parked in my usual place and started the same pattern that Pete and I had walked. But now I moved at a crawl, looking for anything, broken twigs or branches, footprints where the ground was open.

The sun came up in a clear sky, it grew warm, and the woods began to dry quickly. Back and forth I walked between the water and the conservation land on the other side. I checked the ravine carefully and the wide trail but there were no footprints of any kind.

Past the trail, the land began to flatten toward the ocean beaches, but the walking was hard, with the pucker brush dragging at my shins, and I was sweating hard but I kept at it, knowing that once I had finished walking from side to side, I still had to walk it from front to back, in a grid no wider than about twenty feet.

It seemed like a good idea, but even using the compass to hold the squares to about twenty feet, I knew I would need to walk another pattern, a diagonal which would cut through the squares.

I tried not to think of what lay ahead, focusing on what was around me, and at the same time I tried to stay aware of larger elements like hills and valleys.

Moving that way, keeping as quiet as possible, I jumped deer after deer. I had no idea whether they were the same deer or not and I guess probably some of them were, but I had never seen so many. And there were rabbits nearly everywhere.

I stopped frequently to listen, but mostly I only heard the birds and the gulls out by the water. And then, about twenty yards from my last turn in the back-and-forth pattern I spotted a deep sort of gully and I went over to have a look.

The brush was thick and the trees, because I was on the ocean end of the property, were stunted and the branches hung low to the ground. It would be tough walking down there with the brush and having to stoop beneath the trees and I decided to circle it from above first. I made one pass, stopped and reversed direction, remembering having read somewhere that any woods looks different from the opposite direction.

I hadn't gone twenty feet before I stopped and stared down into the ravine. At first I didn't know what I was looking at and then as I shifted from one side to the other I could make it out. A boot. A very large boot.

I held the shotgun in the ready position, the safety on, the barrel up and to the left so I could shoulder the gun quickly. And then I began easing down into the ravine. It was maybe ten or twelve feet deep but, man, was it thick.

I stopped and looked at the boot and then up ahead I saw another and I walked in that direction and stopped.

The body had been torn apart. Arms and legs lay here and there and the back showed great deep slash marks. It looked like it had been there for some time, but in the matter of forensics, things like knowing how long someone has been dead, I was a long way from knowledge.

I can tell you this, though. It was, all in all, about as ugly as anything I'd ever seen and my first thought was to get out of there and call Chief Espinoza.

Curiosity can help you overcome a lot of things, even odor, and that was a good thing because the stench was strong and foul and as I looked I could see flies crawling every-where. There were maggots too.

And then I began to notice other things. Each of the legs was attached to a stilt about a foot and half long. One of the arms ended in big bear paw and it looked as if the claws had been replaced with some sort of sharpened blades.

Nearby, in a pile, lay what looked like a hide stripped from a bear. And bit by bit, things fell into place. But what did not fall into place was who had killed him. Of course, I had a pretty good idea and I began checking the ground. It didn't take long. The huge, clawed footprints were pretty well hidden, but when you pulled the brush apart you could see where the claws had slashed though the years of fallen leaves and twigs on the forest floor.

I smoothed the paw prints out and I took some time to make sure I got them all. Then I climbed up out of the ravine, took out my GPS locator and marked the location. I was pretty sure I could find it easily enough, but I still had a lot to learn about finding things in the woods.

And then I knew he was there, and not very far away and I stood quietly and looked off through the woods. I turned very slowly, letting my eyes look between the trees as far as I could see, but the best I could come up with was a spot about fifty feet away that seemed darker than the surrounding forest.

It could have been a shadow cast by another tree. It could have been nothing more than a different sort of tree. Mostly, it could have been nothing more than my imagination.

Slowly, the feeling faded and I scanned again off to my right and when I looked back the shadow was gone. Which should have been evidence enough, but it wasn't. Light through the trees can easily create illusions, and when you want to see something, you can convince yourself that you've been successful.

For the time being I let go of all that, turned and cut a straight line back to my truck, unloaded the shotgun, stuffed it into its case and put it on the back floor beneath a blanket.

Then I called Chief Espinoza and told him what I'd found and told him I'd be waiting at Mrs. Park's.

He arrived with a full armada, including the coroner and an ambulance and a host of EMT's and cops.

He climbed out of his car and walked over to where I

stood, leaning against my truck.

He grinned and shook his head, took off his ball cap and scratched his head and then screwed the cap back into place.

"I don't know what to make of you, Charlie."

The fact that he was smiling helped. Otherwise a comment like that can go either way, I mean, you're in trouble or you're not.

"Let me see if I've counted right. In about three weeks, you've caught a killer ... twice, and broken a money laundering operation, and you've been playing football at a whole 'nother level. What I want to know here is if things can be expected to keep going this way or will they slow down?"

"Sometimes things just fall into place," I said.

"I'm betting that this body you found was part of the money laundering operation, is that right?"

"Be my guess."

"Why?"

"You'll see when you see what's there and then remember that Mrs. Parks had me here watching the house."

"Just so I'm ahead of the curve a little, can you tell me what's likely to go down next?"

I grinned. "It's Derby time. I'm going fishing."

"And no doubt you expect to win this year."

"Not likely. I catch a lot of fish, but I never seem to get the big ones. I'd put my money on Rob English. Nobody knows where the fish are better than he does."

"But he's never won the Derby."

"He will now."

"You're sure of that."

"He's not the same guy he used to be, you know. Now, he is really intense."

"Which is something you'd be likely to recognize."

"Sure."

`"Well, I guess we ought to get started. You want to lead the way?"

Later, I called Pete and we went out to East Beach on Chappy to see if we couldn't find a fish that would challenge whatever Rob caught. The afternoon was clear and warm and we were there at the start of the incoming tide.

I told him about what I'd found and at first he thought I was putting him on. I decided not to tell him about the sasquatch.

Some things are not meant to be disturbed.